COYOTE GIRL

COYOTE GIRL

Stories

by
Sabrina Hicks

Cowboy Jamboree Press
good grit lit.

Copyright © 2026 by Sabrina Hicks

All rights reserved. No part of this book may be reproduced or used in any manner without written permission of the copyright owner except for the use of quotations in a book review. Rights revert to authors of individual pieces upon publication. For more information, address: cowboyjamboree@gmail.com

First Edition
ISBN: 979-8-90243-176-3

Cover Design: Adam Van Winkle
Interior Design: Adam Van Winkle

Cowboy Jamboree Press
good grit lit.

www.cowboyjamboreemagazine.com/books

Praise for Sabrina Hicks and *Coyote Girl*

"Bull riders measure their whole lives in eight seconds. In that heartbeat between the gate swinging wide and the go's end, bones shatter, tendons snap, and fortunes and futures are made and lost. In *Coyote Girl*, Sabrina Hicks harnesses that same intensity in forty unsparing, mostly flash fictions. Here are drowned children and mangled cowboys rebuilt with titanium. Here is a woman who would rather sling guns than anything else her limited world can offer. Here are lonely diners and desert brushfires and little girls fleeing broken homes to be raised by the wild, both outside and within. Here, Hicks announces herself as a writer you shouldn't and won't and can't ignore."

–Jonathan Danielson, *The Lowest Basin: Arizona Stories*

"Sabrina Hicks' *Coyote Girl* captures the violent beauty of life in the Sonoran Desert: its landscape and its people. With prose that often reads like poetry, this is a love letter to the gorgeous and harsh conditions of the West. The characters in these stories were raised by the sun, chewed up by the heat, and consumed by the flash floods. *Coyote Girl* wants us to think about who we are in relation to where we're from, and it's a divine rumination."

–Stephanie Austin, author of *BURN*

"Sabrina Hicks' story collection, *Coyote Girl*, shines as bright as the high desert sun, displaying all the evocative and polished brilliance this writer possesses, most notably with her women characters, many with warrior spirits, even those in the throes of loneliness and violence, rising up in moments of redemption and liberation. These flash fictions and stories take place in the very unique and emblematic settings: a lonesome desert highway simmering under the noonday heat, the bramble landscape just off the asphalt and thorny arroyos just over the hill turn into life's struggles or salvation, a tree fort which holds, for our time, an essential act of humanity, and a stranded school bus where a connection becomes a lesson worth holding onto. Hicks is a natural-born storyteller, showcasing her deftness with words full of striking images, unforgettable characters, and grace. *Coyote Girl* is a magnificent debut by an author fully flourishing a powerful talent and craft."

–Dan Crawley, author of *Blur*

"This is the book that should be in every hotel room drawer across the American West. Sabrina Hicks is a master of short fiction, and even the shortest of these stories will stick with you long after you've read them. Pick any one of them and let it affect you. When brought together, this collection paints an incredibly deep portrait of a culture and a landscape. Hicks has a knack for writing fierce characters in the throes of hope, grief, and fear, and depicting a sense of yearning that comes to feel inherent to the haunting beauty of the Southwest. For fans of Sam Shepard, Bonnie Jo Campbell, and palo verde trees."

–Burke De Boer, author of *Songs of the Cyberspace Cattle Drive*

"The desert is not only a place but a state-of-mind in *Coyote Girl,* Sabrina Hicks' remarkable collection of stories. Hicks' characters are seemingly as desolate as the desert they inhabit but there is beauty and strength in their stories that left me gasping in admiration. With hints of magic, stunning imagery, and unique and devastating insight into the human condition, this is one of the best story collections I have ever read. Highly recommended."

–Barbara Byar, author of *In the Desert*

HEREIN

For my mother.

Eight Seconds

I saw the ghost of you riding the fence line of our old ranch, your sad eyes under a cowboy hat, lips set like a half-bent fishing line, same as when you told me you wanted to become a bronc rider in the rodeo—eight seconds with one hand wedged between hide and rope, the other waving in the air like that old blue ribbon tied to your truck. You looked the same as every picture of your childhood, head bent so low all anyone could see of you was a cowboy on a half-broke horse, moving cattle to the pasture with the tallest grass and highest water tank, where the land wasn't so parched, waiting on a rain that passed as quickly as it came before that whiskey sun poured thick over the mesas, painting an uneven sky. The thing is Dad always needed you—some old maverick got stuck in a knot of manzanitas, a mountain lion gutted a calf, a horse broke its leg in barbed wire, and off you'd go and home I stayed because that's what girls did then—we stayed—and the day you didn't come back, I rode out to our favorite spot, the cliff overlooking a stretch of land so far and wide you could forget you were becoming our old man, and I was becoming a girl set on leaving. And while not one ranch-hand could find you, I found your horse saddled, eating sage, you at the bottom of the ravine with your neck snapped, and my God, how I hated you for leaving me, for dying in such a foolish way, wondering what you were doing along that mountain road alone, riding the cliff's edge when you'd been having more and more seizures. *Don't tell anyone,* you made me promise, knowing we had a mother who only believed in the power of prayer and a father who'd never give his boy the eight seconds of feeling his heart rise in his chest and take flight. I wish you could have seen me ride out and never look back. I wish you could have come with. I wish you knew I'd give it all up for you to have your eight seconds with your head held high drinking in that whiskey sun.

Sabrina Hicks

All Water Holds a Memory

The prickly pear fruit stained everything red—fingers, our clothes, the air. Our stomachs louder than the thunderclap, that maw inside us, clawing like root sprawl until the sky broke. A year older than you, I was used to dropping to the desert floor, ear to sand, listening for the pulse of water. I saw you'd followed me into the dry wash only after I climbed the limbs of a cottonwood. You stood for a second—my slack-jawed baby brother, looking up at me just before a river raged between us. I remember that first rush of water, a scream inside me, filling my lungs where it would stay.

Every night I went to the riverbed trying to make sense of where you were, swept away from the one thing we desired, the one thing this town prayed for. You and I would grab our rain sticks and dance in front of our ranch house with an audience of mountains and cattle, sagebrush and junipers, the desert floor slick with lavender berries we'd break open, inhaling gin. We'd stagger around, bury fistfuls in our pockets knowing Ma would curse us on laundry day. We'd fill hollowed-out wood with them, drive nails into the sides after Dad told us the sound of rain is mimicked when the beans fall through thorns.

When it rains, I hear your voice. I am back on the swollen riverbank, lying beside you, our bloated bellies sloshing as we shift side to side, our mother's words ringing in our ears. *Listen for the sky. Watch for each other. Come home.* The thought of death kept us alive, but that aliveness is when death comes. No day arrives without night. Your bones were carried miles away, covered in juniper-blue—lupines and African daisies, surrounded by the signs of what would be our most generous spring.

Cowboy Titanium

I told the cops I didn't know Dale was going to rob the Mountainaire Mini Mart. Only found $78 on Dale's close-to-dying body after the cashier shot him in the back. I could've told him it wouldn't be worth his time, that nobody carried cash no more. As far as I knew, he was putting 15 dollars' worth of diesel in his truck and buying me a pack of Kools, though I don't think he had enough money for tax on the smokes, seeing how the state is trying to break everybody of their bad habits, just like Mama tried to break me of my Dale habit. Dale rode the rodeo, wore a big ol' belt buckle and cowboy hat, kept his rifle racked in the back window of his Chevy next to his Blue Lives Matter sticker—insurance he called it. He'd been working at the Piney Peak Mine for the last year, a job that wasn't paying the hospital bills he'd accumulated on account of his bull riding days, said he was more titanium than man after his surgeries and would stick to broncs. Said he couldn't go through metal detectors. Said magnets stuck to his body. *I'm made of steel, baby! Cowboy titanium!* Made me call him The Terminator when we started dating, all 150 pounds of him. He came from west Texas, what he called God fearing country, though after visiting his mama in that dust town, I only saw fear, no sign of God. Dale didn't die that day. The clerk who shot him hit a metal plate deep inside him. Titanium saved him. No God in that neither. What saved me was the bullet that finally found the soft fleshy part of his organs after he held me down screaming at me to call him The Terminator. I reckon I broke my Dale habit that night. Haven't had a smoke since neither.

Sabrina Hicks

Synonyms for Extraction

Merriam Webster: ancestry, birth, blood, bloodline, breeding, descent, family tree, genealogy, line, lineage, origin, parentage, pedigree, stock, strain

At ten, I pulled a baby calf from its mother's womb, elbow deep in warm birthing fluids, feeling limbs and heat, matted fur and flesh, the beating pulse of a life with no desire to enter the world. *Grab 'em from the underside, Callie, and pull with everything you have,* my mother instructed. *Don't worry about being gentle. Just get her out.* After that, I always helped alongside my mother, trying to better understand her, a woman who above all else, relished all types of extractions: births, blemishes, thorns, a growing abscess from an ingrown hair infecting the tailbone of my older brother from riding too long on horseback.

In the evening, she'd squeeze and pack Devon's wound with ice secretly hoping it would fill again so she would have something to extract the next day. She'd scan our growing bodies, eye our blemishes, wait for calls from other farmers and ranchers needing her assistance in animal husbandry and difficult labors. *Get Carol. She and her daughter can bring anything into this world.* They'd say this, even knowing she'd lost a child, my twin in fact, in a water tank outside the corral.

They say it doesn't take much water for a child to drown. It only took a foot and a half for my twin sister, Meg. We were two years old at the time. My father was in the barn fixing his saddle while my sister and I were taking fistfuls of hay to feed the horses. Maybe Meg tried to palm the water and give the animals a drink. Maybe I pushed her in. No one knew as my mother came down the road from town and saw me staring into the tank where my sister floated face down. In my dreams, I see her face—a moonlit cherub with golden hair, my mother extracting her limp body from the water with the same look she has when she is forcing something into this world and has forgotten how to breathe, as if remembering will kill her.

Sabrina Hicks

Little Lady

I've been here before, gunslinging in the bottom of a dust bowl, surrounded by prairie sprawl wrapped in a rim of mountains. I bend down, roll a handful of dirt in my sweaty palms, press the pebbles deep, catch the remnants of a bottle thrown from the corner saloon, a shard of glass I squeeze tight. The blood helps the grit stick.

I check the clock, hear it strike twelve. It's always high noon. They call me little lady behind my back. But if they say it to my face, I liquor them up, purr in their ear, tell 'em to meet me in the center of town and when they do, they come laughing until I sink a bullet in their gut, turn their laughter into surprise, and surprised is how they die. Winner takes all. That's what keeps me gunslinging and not dancing on a stage, tits out in a frilly dress staring into the eyes of men, or teaching children in a one room school house because I ain't interested in being respectable and I ain't interested in being a whore and those are the only two options in this one-horse town, so I created a third.

This man I've seen a hundred times, smug and self-righteous, so sure of his place in this world before I displace him. He smiles at me. I blow him a kiss. The audience calls it the kiss of death. They love a good show, helps them forget their lives for a flash, to watch and jeer before going back to their shop-keeping and banking, drinking and leaning on wooden posts with toothpicks between their teeth like they're on a movie set because they are. We all are. The least we can do is choose our role.

"I can't shoot a woman," says the man who had no problem sticking his whiskey tongue in my ear, pinching my ass as I hitched my horse to a tree last night. The same man I caught forcing himself on one of the dancers. The same man every time.

"Then this shouldn't take long," I say.

My younger sister found the Lord and doesn't approve of my life choices. Tries to appeal to my softer side, but my softer side is leather not lace. She tells me I wouldn't be able to live with myself, but I'm living just fine. I tell her maybe I had a heart a long time ago, but it's long gone cause I feel nothing for these men I purge. She says, *remember Daddy, how he tried to do right by us when Mama died.* But the man I remember showed me how to quickdraw, how to clean a gun, how to stare evil in the eye and spit back. Told me I should've been born a son. Told me it's a man's world, trust no one, and to hide my beauty cause it ain't worth the trouble. Then he kicked me out saying I wasn't welcome back unless I made something of myself.

The man before me has no interest in abiding by the rules we'd set forth: the meeting of our backs, the walking of paces, the heel toe heel toe of suspense. He wants to get right to the action, right to the moment of death and surprise, wants to know what I whisper in their ear as they beg for their Lord, their mama, their life. The rumors are I say, *see you in hell,* tell 'em a secret I don't tell anyone, say, *bang bang motherfucker*.

But no matter how many times I've been at this, they all have the same scolded schoolboy look so I don't vary the script. I whisper: *Call me little lady one more time.* And then I wait. Not one of them took me up on this offer. And this man standing before me, quietly shaking in his boots, hand going for his piece but not nearly in time, won't either. Soon he'll know his place.

Sabrina Hicks

When the Cowboy Separates the Calves for Tomorrow's Branding

the mothers will bawl in the pastures, their babies will huddle together in the pens, the cowboy will remember his mother leaving, his daddy whipping him for being inconsolable.

When the cowboy separates the calves for tomorrow's branding, the cowboy's wife knows he will drink too much whiskey, will cry out in his sleep, will wake to the bawling outside their window, pull a pillow over his head, say, *I'm going to whip their hide.*

When the cowboy separates the calves for tomorrow's branding, the cowboy will learn he'll become a father, later learn it's a son, later learn his cries, know that he himself is haunted.

But for now, babies by their sides, the cows are quiet and content, heads buried in the thick sweet-grass; and the cowboy and his wife wake to birdsong, wake in an embrace, wake with a sliver of sunlight stretching across their quilted bed.

Memorial of Imaginary Lines

When I order at the diner in the desert, I point to the picture of two perfectly round eggs on a piece of petrified toast, thinking about the roadside memorial I passed turning into the parking lot – a melted shrine, colored a sick gray, consisting of a stuffed creature with sun-singed hair, leaning against a cross of plastic flowers — a small gesture of remembrance becoming a stain in the grout of earth.

"Coffee, miss?" asks the server, wearing a costume of what a waitress at a diner would have worn decades earlier – knee length, flared pink skirt and white blouse. She's too old for the outfit, but somehow it suits her. I look around and realize the entire diner is a throwback to another day and age. A Before.

The waxed memory of the memorial leaves me speechless. I shake my head, loosening my tongue. "Who died on the corner coming in here?"

The server shrugs, deciding what to tell a stranger passing through this small town. I can tell she knows.

"Jackson McCabe," she sighs. "He hit the post after leaving The Oasis."

"Was he drunk?"

She stares at me, holding the pot of coffee over my cup, resisting the pour. If he was drunk, his tragedy is downgraded to a reckless decision, wielding a deadly weapon. I can see her weighing this, part mad I'm asking, part mad about the truth.

"Where're you heading?" she asks, opting for a distraction.

I'm in Arizona, but I could be heading to Utah, Colorado or New Mexico, depending how I drive out of here. I have Colorado locked into my GPS, a route leading to my sister's house where I will walk in and find my three nieces. I haven't been there for years, but I remember the sweet smell of their rooms, each a different bloom woven into a house full of women. Photos line the ledges: her girls smiling on California beaches, in Europe, on campuses of the schools they're attending in the fall. There may even be one of Sasha mixed in with her cousins, and then I might forget how to breathe.

"I don't know," I say, which I realize is the truth. Last year, I didn't make it this far. I only got two hours out of Phoenix before I turned around. I think I should feel a sense of accomplishment, but I don't. I only feel the strong tug back.

"I thought you might be heading to the Four Corners. It's only twenty minutes away. People love standing on that plaque of imaginary lines."

I look at the nametag of my server – Claire. She winks at me, and I think she knows, but then again, all acts of kindness feel this way. She combs back her gum gray hair gathered in a thick bun, takes my menu, and disappears into the kitchen.

Outside the day is bone white and one hundred and eleven degrees. People walk in red-faced and sweating, complaining about the heat, the lack of rain, about how their car batteries are melting in their garages where scorpions linger under a collection of bicycles and coolers and bins stuffed with camping gear, and I resist doing that scene that has played out in my mind every day for the last three years where I stand up and scream as loud as I can until all the words around me have vanished and there is nothing but silence and the face of Sasha before she turns to get behind the wheel of her aqua green 2014 Honda Civic. Before she pulls away with a wave and says, "Bye, Mom," in a voice that says I'm overprotective. Before the boozy driver of the 2011 Ford Ranger runs the light and pins her to that corner of the intersection where she takes her final breath. Before my life had an After.

Claire returns with a plate of eggs and a smile that feels intimate. "Fuel for your journey," she says.

I eat, watching Claire work the tables, slinging plates with her thick arms, chatting up the customers, but her eyes seem to linger on me and it puts a lump in my throat, making it difficult to swallow the already dry eggs.

Outside the cicadas shriek as I make my way to my car. I sit behind the wheel until I can no longer stand the heat, then pull up to the stop sign, next to the melting memorial for Jackson McCabe, following my GPS, heading north on 160, crossing the Four Corners into Colorado.

Sabrina Hicks

Fire Season

Our neighborhood woke like a hive, gathering outside, huddling around each other's yards. *It's been dry*. Heads nod. *No rain*. Heads shake. But it's April in the desert and the monsoons are still a few months away. The sun beats down, a wedge of lemon-yellow sliced high in a corner, and on the ground, a dusty sepia as a new fire streaks down the mountain coming for us, opening like a wound, licking the last of the creosote green. My brother is nowhere to be found. No one says what they're thinking. My brother: combing the dry desert washes, throwing rocks, howling along with the new neighbor kid who'd been through a rotation of schools, the one who will be sent to military school a month later to avoid suspicion.

The retired school teacher two houses down, the one with the Jesus fish hammered into his front door, pushes up thick glasses, tries to sound casual, *Where's your brother?* Then a beat later, *And his friend?* They don't ask my mother, who is squatting low on the edge of our yard, thumbing a green oleander leaf with so much distance in her eyes she's already gone. *I don't know*, I say, and it's the truth, but it isn't the whole truth because the truth is he has a drawer full of matchbooks from the restaurants and motels where my father used to take women who weren't our mother. My brother picked our father's pockets before he left for good: matches, mints, and money. That may have been the spark, but my brother has always been drawn to a flame and everyone knows it. But they have no proof and he isn't here and neither is that new kid he hangs out with, the one whose father is off right now on a military assignment. And the kid's mother isn't here either, but we'll learn later she's at the school, head between the principal's knees, trying to prevent her son from getting kicked out again, and my brother is hiding in the desert somewhere with him, planning an escape, wearing the tactical gear of men on an assignment, and I'm doing cartwheels on the one patch of dying grass in this desert town, readying myself for another run, working in calf stretches and lunges knowing there's nothing left for us here, and we'll move soon like the last time my brother lit a fire, and I wonder if that's what my mother and I wait for, these little fires, trying to outrun the flames of men and boys and little desert towns, toward a small patch of something green.

Sabrina Hicks

Carriage

The sun touches everything in the morning, filtering its light though the polyester curtains made to look like lace, hitting the toilet's porcelain curve, bending into water clotted with blood that has slipped from my body like an inevitable hiccup.

On the ground, I straddle the bowl, stir the color with my fingertips—battlefield red turning a soft pink.

"Come now, Maisie," my mother says.

I am too consumed memorializing Rose, certain she would've had my auburn hair and Ben's soft lips. They're all Roses now. Rose 1 was years ago. This is Rose 5.

"Maisie," she soothes, sitting on the floor behind me, pulling me into an embrace. I breathe in the scent of her: sun, lavender, and childhood. "Ben called me. Told me you've been in here for hours."

After Rose 2, Ben always calls her. I don't blame him. It's my body that has rejected us, and the weight of that burden is one I cannot seem to share.

Her eyes are watery wishing wells. Her skin, settling into post middle age, now mapped with detours and a painful familiar history. She has been here before, on the same baby blue tile, stroking my hair, preaching the hollow words of God's will. Thankfully she isn't doing that. I don't believe in God—not for a while now. Instead she starts humming. It takes me a minute to recognize the Judy Collins song. Then when I do, I return to the silence buzzing in my ear, a calm pulse inside me, rivers of blood feeding me oxygen.

She reaches for the handle to flush and I stop her, inhaling the sweet iron.

I don't know how my life became so myopic. I try to remember when I wanted other things, when life's trajectory wasn't linear: school, career, marriage, children. I was a list maker, checking off the first three with little effort, and now, the latter is unraveling them all. Ben has run out of words. My office, out of patience. My mind whittled down to one goal, so sharp it feels like the days are lined with broken glass. Today I am memorializing even longer, and something is different, though I can't imagine what when this has become routine.

My mother shushes my thoughts and I wonder if I have spoken them aloud when she tells me it's not the end. *Not the end* echoes as if I've fallen down a cliff. But my mother only wishes to soothe. When this doesn't work, she'll take a firm approach—insist I soldier on. I picture her behind me lifting me under my arms as we trudge through foreign land together with gunfire at our backs. "Get up! Keep moving!" Until the steps become my own.

Though my mother isn't speaking, I know time is passing. Sunlight moves from the toilet to my knees. My skin is pale and in need of a shave. It shifts slowly to my mother's thicker body. She is wearing leggings and a floral top and is holding me like she's trying to keep my insides from spilling out. She leans against the wall with the window above us. So much time is passing that the bathroom becomes our universe, my mother becomes the sun, I orbit her, and my unborn babies are the moons orbiting us both. Nothing else seems to exist until I hear Ben ask us if we're all right on the other side of the locked door.

"In time," my mother responds, and it feels so true that I lean over and flush. The toilet swirls then swallows, and I'm back in her arms, listening to the water snake through the pipes in the walls. I feel so small, like I'm crawling back into her womb. There are no words to stop me, and the silence is cradling us both. She goes back to humming, and I go to sleep in her arms just to pass the time, so I can begin again.

Sabrina Hicks

Coyote Girl

When I was five, I walked out our patio door that backed up to the mountain foothills and got lost in the desert for four days and three nights. I was found ten miles away in a sandy wash, in between a couple of boulders, and for weeks I was a local media sensation: nightly news, helicopters, search crews, homemade cards from my kindergarten class, including Mrs. Maggiano, a teacher who'd showed no fondness for me prior to my disappearance. When asked if I'd remembered anything I would say it felt like a dream, like fragments of a puzzle I couldn't quite piece together.

My mother would recite the story at dinner parties, whenever there was a need for interesting conversation. Maybe she tried to disarm the gossipers and get ahead of the story, relieve some of her guilt, but after a decade or so, each retelling began to sound more like a dark fairytale. She'd be buying a pair of earrings at a department store, lean into the salesperson with a conspiratorial whisper, *Sadie was abducted by coyotes when she was five. Even howled like them, too*. The conversation always ending with, *She could've died out there all alone. Instead, she became a wolf.*

When I returned to school, I told my classmates I was half coyote, that I was raised by a pack. I'd howl until they believed me. I'd howl and be sent to the principal's office. I'd howl under full moons, when my parents began arguing, when I had no words for the loneliness I harbored throughout my childhood. I howled for reasons I still don't understand.

My parents finally divorced when I was ten, which left me—with my mother's face—in her custody; and my brothers—with his face—in my dad's custody. I know my father would have left sooner if I hadn't put a spotlight on my family. For a while, no one trusted their kids to come over and play at my house. There were rumors my mother was a day drinker, a pill popper. Why else would it take her seven hours to file a report? How did she not know her daughter was missing? The police were called when my father came home from work. It was getting dark and he asked, *Where's Sadie?* And my mother, head buried in a book, dishes in the sink, my brothers playing tackle football outside, waved him off and said, *Probably in her room or with the boys.*

I bought my mother five more years with a man she didn't love, who didn't love her back. I bought five more wasted years.

The press called me Coyote Girl, and so did my classmates, after a comment I made about following the coyotes to find water. They'd whisper it before the bell rang, in the halls, in the bathroom just as I'd enter a stall. I'd pick up my feet, hear a new pack of girls say, *Coyote Girl must be in here, it smells like wolf crap. She howls, you know. She goes into the desert at night to visit them.* And then I'd howl and scare the shit out of them. I'd howl until I was alone in the bathroom with my eyes closed, imagining those nights in the desert, how the stars appeared chiseled into the slate black sky, the moon casting its blue light, softening the cacti and dry brush. How it felt like all anyone needed in this world to survive was a small sliver of moonlight.

When dad left us, I found mom wedged between her bed and nightstand, where she thought no one would find her. I curled up with her, put my ear to her heart to hear it beat. She cried long and slow, like a cub when she needed to howl. So I howled for her, for her generation that mistook suffering for strength and silence for grit. Then she said so quietly I thought I imagined it, *You could have died out there.*

That was the last time I howled—as a child.

I moved three states away, where no one had ever heard of Coyote Girl, and I stayed there until my mother grew old, until she needed me to come home. She started to forget where the car keys were, the passcodes for everything, how a flame on a stovetop needed to be watched. But oddly, she recalled the day I went missing with startling clarity, remembering the smallest of details.

"Sadie, you wore that green corduroy coat the day you disappeared. It had a little rainbow on its collar and a torn pocket.

Do you remember when you came back you thought you were a coyote? You'd sniff all your meals; you tried eating raw meat."

"Yes, Ma."

"In those days, kids used to play outside until it was dark. In those days, kids were independent—none of this technology or twenty-four-hour entertainment to babysit."

"And that's how latchkey kids ended up with their pictures on milk cartons."

She waved me off. "The day you left was the day I knew your father was cheating on me."

"Oh," I said. What do you say to a secret you already knew?

She grabbed my hand. "I was so distracted, so distraught, you could have died."

"But I didn't, Ma. I didn't."

"Not just the time you were gone. I mean all the little deaths that come with living every day. You were always more alive than anyone. You saw things no one else did."

And I wondered if she knew, had always known the real story of why I'd walked deep into the desert when I was little, that I'd heard my father arguing with her that morning, saying he wanted to leave her and I thought if I left them both, they would find me—together. But then I got lost for real as I wandered down the dry riverbeds, kicking sand and stones, snapping off branches of palo verdes, and by night I made myself small like a rock, like in that book my mother would read to me where a donkey named Sylvester had a magic pebble and wished he was a rock when confronted with a hungry lion. And so, I found the biggest boulders I could and hid between them, thinking my parents would find me, they'd feel bad about losing me, losing each other, and I'd have my wish.

On the first night I went missing, a light rain fell, and I no longer cared about the plan, about the wish. I was hungry and thirsty and lost, and all I wanted was my mother. A pack of coyotes wandered down the wash, looking for pockets of water. I saw where they drank and followed their movements, and at night, they'd come back and sniff around me, paw at the boulders, howling for hours as I wedged myself further and further into a stone crevice.

After that first night, I wasn't afraid of the coyotes. I howled with them, straight up at the moon. I howled so long and hard it chased all the fear out of me until there was nothing left but longing and regret and a small sense of peace. Later, I was found by the sheriff's dog who'd sniffed me out ahead of a search party.

"Do you still howl?"

"No, Ma. I'm a grown woman."

"That shouldn't matter," she said. "We should howl and get lost and find ourselves again and again."

She closed her eyes and a nurse came to say her visiting hours were almost over, but I could stay the night if I wanted. My mother didn't have much time left. Her vitals weren't good. She had survived a stroke, a fall, a bout of cancer, the gradual breakdown of her body. After my mother fell asleep, I lay beside her on the hospital bed, hearing her breath slow into a shallow rattle. I tried remembering the story about the donkey, about how lonely he was until he was found. But I had no words inside me. No words to convey the growing ache. As her breath grew quiet and I held her in my arms, I only felt the stabbing slip of a slow and mournful howl.

Sabrina Hicks

Potential

In junior high, I took up palm reading. I wanted to know what the world had in store for me and everyone I came in contact with. I bought books, watched YouTube videos, sketched diagrams into the night, then I'd reach for the soft hands of my classmates before the bell rang, trace the lines in their palms with my finger and say things like: *you will have a long life; you will get married at 28; you will come into money, but only briefly because you divorce three times you whore, ha-ha.*

Sometimes I'd spin long and sordid tales, but I knew the lengths and intersections of the lines, the direction of their meaning—though I never let the truth get in the way. And the kids would line up like I knew things, like I had answers. I was a fraud, of course, because I believed in potential over fate. Fate had only given me a small life, in a small town, and I was determined to take over, widen my circle, make my own fate, thinking all my friendships and love interests were most likely ones born out of convenience, proximity, comfort.

I could find an excuse to pick up the inky hand of the poet in my English class, two rows away, a boy who wrote dark poems in his notebook, on every side margin, no white space to be had, words soaring off the page onto his skin. A boy who by the end of our high school years, would drive to a big city, find a bridge, and jump. I held his hand, saw the shortness of his lines, the crazy dissections, the fractured groves marking past trauma. I wanted to take his pen and redraw the lines into wings. *What?* he said. *No good?* I slowly traced the broken bits like I was trying to connect and repair them. Then I put my palm on top of his and told him I saw potential. *So much fucking potential.*

Farrago

I stood in line to pay for my cart of groceries exhausted from working at the pharmacy, sorting pills for people who need them, people who think they need them, and some looking to fix what is broken and beyond repair, and in line is a woman I once knew, a friend from pharmacy school who dropped out and went to Paris instead because Paris is a different kind of prescription. Paris is wine and cafes along the Seine. And this woman I knew, who is now a stranger, has unloaded her frozen meals and potato chips and boxed white wine and I think I should say something to her because I had known her once a long time ago; I knew her favorite candy were those terrible circus peanuts that tasted like foam and sugar; I knew she slept with Kevin O'Malley and regretted it enough to cry and make me wonder if it was consensual, and when I pushed, perhaps too hard, I was sure there hadn't been any consent, and was even more sure she resented me for leading her to that obvious conclusion. I knew, too, that she drank too much Diet Coke, and later, rum and Diet Coke (though I see neither in her cart now) and snapped Trident gum (also not in her cart) and didn't watch enough movies to know when I was quoting Jaws or Moonstruck or any movie for that matter. I'm thinking of all this when she catches me staring at the items she has chosen, and then at her, and I am dizzy and off balance at the knowing and not knowing of her, the intimacy and the void. There's terrible music playing throughout the store, a song that is only terrible because it's been played enough to become background noise in soul-crushing stores saturated in fluorescent lights and people tired from life and repetition, flanked by tabloid trash and gift cards to box stores that keep people on the wheel. *Hey, Meg,* she says, taking in my face, its age and wrinkles, my scrubs that I wear, my cart full of processed sugar and protein shakes and basically anything that doesn't come from a recognizable tree or crop or even animal, and I am both embarrassed and relieved. I open my mouth but before I can say anything the clerk has dismissed her and her groceries, threatening her with *have a nice evening* and the bagger is pulling away her cart of boxed wine and frozen entrees and all I can get out is *How was France?* And for a few seconds she is somewhere far away and I'm with her on this small escape, we all are because everyone's eyes are on our exchange as if she'd just gotten back and it hadn't been 16 years ago. *Trés bien,* she says, smiling widely and I smile back, an honest smile because I'm happy for her. *It's good to see you,* I say. And then we let each other go back to our lives of processed sugar and boxed wine, pinched dreams and those nights we'd rather forget, and I find myself humming the song still playing about finding our reflections and turning around and so too is the clerk and bagger, and we exchange small smiles and pleasantries and genuine excitement over the coming weekend.

Object Permanence

My sister got a half-heart tattoo on her wrist, said the other half was with one of those dirt bike boys outside the 7-11, begging for booze, moving on to petty crime, and is someone she thinks is worth a visit today at the county jail. I picture Daisy in there behind the glass partition in her new yellow lace top, tapping her chewed nails with chipped blue polish while I sun myself in the old Pontiac convertible Mom left us. I'd stopped reading the book I'd found on the dash, and had tipped my seat way back so I could no longer see the chain link fence or the coiled razor wire of the prison yard. All I see is big sky with a stitch of white from a plane going somewhere I imagine a lot of green, or a white sand beach with a sway of trees. A place that erases everything.

When she comes back, she slings her purse to the floor by my feet.

"Took you long enough," I say, though I enjoyed being alone with the sky.

"He's a piece of shit," Daisy says.

I want to ask which one again when they're all the same version of our deadbeat father. I want to tell her I love her, but we haven't said those words since Mom died a year ago and now they feel too much of what holds us together.

"Cee Cee!" she snaps, gesturing for me to sit up.

I launch my seat upright until my view is an assault of serrated metal wrapped around acres of dead grass and blocks of concrete buildings.

"He begged me to come," she yells over the engine, adjusting the rearview mirror. "Said he had some really big news and the big news is he needs money for a lawyer."

I look at the side of her: hair combed long and straight, face painted. She looks like our mother and it strikes me she's the same age as Mom was when she had Daisy—twenty years old, five years older than me and now my legal guardian. On nights I can't sleep she lets me call her Mama, maybe even strokes my hair, tells me things she'd heard Mom say when we were little, starting over someplace new. *Sweet dreams til sunbeams find you, Cee Cee.*

"Have you ever heard of object permanence?" I ask. She's on the desert road, nothing but cacti and this scar of blacktop leading away from the prison that contains the father of that seed inside Daisy, forming, taking shape into someone I try to imagine, but cannot.

"No," she says, and I can tell she is deciding whether to cry or get mad.

"Babies don't have it, but we do. It's when you understand something is there even when you can't see it."

She eyes the book in my lap. It's the one she left in the car, the one about pregnancy and what to expect, as if the anxiety of what's to come can be tolerated if only the mother believes she can know the unknowable. Daisy's knuckles grow white around the wheel, angry tears run down her face, and the wind is hitting us so our hair is everywhere, turning our view into a mosaic of cacti and road.

"Why are you reading that book?"

"Nothing else to do while I was waiting."

I'm hoping she stays mad, but she's crying and softening and that's worse. I look down at the book, see the mother in a rocking chair, cradling her pregnant belly and think, Mom would know what to do. She'd know and this world took her right when we needed her the most. A lump in her breast, a biopsy, a late stage diagnosis, a year of casseroles, pies, appointments, fundraisers, debt. Then nothing but a house with her ghost in every room.

"When you play peek-a-boo with a baby, they don't know where you go when you cover your face with your hands. Imagine that," I say over the wind. "Imagine the only thing that exists is what we see in front of us right here, right now—this long stretch of road, our horizon ending with those mountains ahead," I gesture to the formation of rocks, washed out under a low winter sun. "Like whatever is happening on the other side in that valley is not happening. Maybe it doesn't even exist until we get there."

Daisy pulls over on the lone highway and our hair falls into knotted piles. There is a thin layer of dust on our faces. I rub the grit away, pull the strands of hair out of my mouth to ask her what she's doing.

"Once we get over those mountains, things change, Cee Cee, and I don't know what to do."

"You didn't tell him, did you?"

She shakes her head no, runs her fingers through her hair, then stares down at her flat stomach.

I extend my hand to hers and give it a squeeze. "Once we get over those mountains, there will be no right answer and there will be no wrong answer. There will only be an imperfect answer. And you'll know what to do because we'll do it together, whatever it is."

Daisy buries her head into my shoulder and I stroke her hair, saying things I know our mother would say. She pulls away and digs around in the cup holder, takes out a pen and puts it to the inside of my wrist, drawing the other half of her tattooed heart. When the ink is bold, we line them up to match and she smiles at me in a way that holds no memory of our mother dying, of Daisy working two jobs to pay our rent, of boys who hurt her. She's just Daisy. And the road ahead will be nothing but air rushing past, mountains in front of us, a memory left behind, and me next to her.

Sabrina Hicks

When We Knew How to Get Lost

Fifty miles out of town, on a road with no name, I hitched a ride after we argued about your Chevy running out of gas (our first argument) and came back with two candy bars as a peace offering, a gallon of fuel, and an old guy named Mitch who ended up knowing your mom and got in a bar fight with your dad once. It was the first time I told you about my family, about the cancer that took my mother.

When spur of the moment we drove the I-10 from Tucson to El Paso because we'd never been to Texas. We dipped our toe in the state, ate at a diner, found out it was an 11-hour drive to Houston, nine to Dallas, and we didn't have that kind of time so we turned around, drove back through the desert singing Johnny Cash songs, eating gas station beef jerky and corn nuts, throwing our heads back to howl at the moon every time we passed a billboard for *The Thing?*—a supposed mystery in the desert that we knew was just a tourist trap of rubber aliens and dinosaurs. That night you told me you couldn't imagine getting lost with anyone else.

When we were going to your older brother's cabin near Flagstaff with unmarked signs and instructions to: *look for a fork in the road, then a tree with a knotted trunk that looks like Steve Buscemi.* We drove past every tree cursing your brother's name until you told me how he protected you from your father's fist, and when I saw your face crumple in pain, I made you stop and held you with the windows open and the smell of pine thick in the air. When we pulled apart I saw Buscemi's face clear as day and yelled, *there!*

When we drove through South Carolina and you were too embarrassed to pull over and ask where the World's Largest Peach was so I stuck my head out the window and shout-sang Peaches by The Presidents of the United States until you did. At the gas station you said you would marry me one day and I said, *only after I find a million of peaches for free!*

When we were trying to find a farmer's market outside of Denver but ended up driving along a mountain that twisted into the clouds. I said, *watch the gas gauge. I doubt your mom knows anyone I can hitch a ride with here, but I sure as hell will run into someone your old man pissed off.* There was an unmarked road we pulled into, and when we walked to the bottom there were two chairs and a lake and a hundred miles of land stretching over a horizon. You said, *who needs a market or money or cars or a home when our eyes can see this. This!* Your arms outstretched. *Who needs anything but this?* We watched the sky ripen around the sun, bruising into evening, not knowing it would be our last time getting lost together, a last time before direction ruined everything.

Sabrina Hicks

Falling Saguaros

When the saguaros began to fall, my mother wrapped shade cloths around the cacti in her yard to protect them from the sun. The desert nights were supposed to cool off, give the plants a chance to recover, but the nights never cooled. Not enough anyway. Some rotted quickly and toppled over; others fell slowly, limb by limb. Mom went to church to pray for them, pray for rain and redemption, pray the heat would break, pray her 26-year-old son would get clean and her two daughters would find Jesus.

The summer of falling saguaros, my brother Jerry stole a car that led to an hour-long police chase, ending in the Arizona desert. He flipped the car and took cover in the Superstition Mountains, a place known to swallow the unprepared. The days that followed were brutal—118-degree heat with no water source meant a junkie like him was as good as dead. Search crews didn't look too hard, not with Jerry's record, and his body was never found.

One of the cops told me the car he'd stolen played Aerosmith's "Livin' on the Edge" on repeat, which felt like Jerry was trying to tell us a message we already knew. Now I can't hear the song when it comes on the radio. I don't know why the officer told me that. I suppose he was offering some detail, or worse, some warning, but if he looked up the lyrics, the warning was for everyone.

My sister, Sarah, and I drove out there after they cleared the wreck and called off the search. She hammered a wooden cross into the hard ground, an unforgiving caliche, sweating like mad.

"We're not even religious," I said.

She shrugged, placing a ring of hot stones around its base while I stood there with an umbrella to shade us.

"Jerry would've hated this," I said, thinking of all the sad crosses we saw along the highway with faded plastic flowers and raggedy stuffed animals. "*I* hate this."

"How I memorialize him isn't his business. It isn't even yours, Marie." Sarah stood, dusting off her jeans. "He may have been my twin, but you were always more like him."

She wasn't wrong. Although they were two years older than me, it felt like Jerry and I were the same person, like all my bad instincts were buried in him, and he lived them out to show me the path not to take.

Mom didn't leave her bedroom after the accident. She stayed in bed watching the local news, waiting for a break in a case that was as good as dead, as if he'd emerge from the desert like a mirage. Sarah and I took turns driving over to her house, sliding trays of food under her locked bedroom door, which meant we had to make pancakes or anything flat enough to fit under a two-and-a-half-inch gap.

"I'm not convinced she's eating, Marie," Sarah said. "But I'm tired of her yelling at me to go to mass."

After a work trip, I went to check on her and discovered her air-conditioning had bit the dust and it was over 100 degrees inside her house. When I finally got through her bedroom door, I found the food my sister and I had made was hard and uneaten, water in her glass slowly evaporating, her lifeless body in bed with her hand stiff around the remote as the news promised rain. She died of dehydration and heat stroke. She died from a broken heart.

Sarah and I buried her a month after Jerry died in the cemetery along the highway. A huge wall surrounded the grounds in an attempt to quiet the traffic, but it didn't work. The priest, Father John, had to shout over a roar of mufflers and engines. He wore a heavy robe during the third hottest day on record and only lasted ten minutes outside before he felt faint. He sat down mid-service looking pale.

As my mother's coffin lay there with flowers drying on top of the polished wood, I imagined her shriveling to dust, the sixty percent of water held in a human body already gone. For a moment, a vehicle must have pulled off the side of the highway and we got a blast of Guns-N-Roses singing "Sweet Child of Mine" on a car stereo. Sarah finally broke down. It had been her favorite song and she saw it as a sign. Maybe it was. Maybe signs, like ghosts, are all around us.

In the cemetery courtyard a fallen saguaro blocked our path on the way out. Father John apologized for the mess, said it had fallen that morning. It'd been watered and cared for. It hadn't died of thirst like the wild ones in the desert. Sometimes we can do everything right and things still fall. We can love and nurture. We can pray and shed light. But light can be turned into fire. Father John said the water in the cactus heated up and boiled its inside. Its 20-foot corpse lay in a face plant with its arms up in surrender, a gash oozing a dark, hot sap on the bricks. We had to step over its thick, spiny flesh with Father John standing by, offering his shaky hand to anyone.

Sarah and I drove out to Jerry's cross in the desert after Mom's service, passing water between us like a bottle of whiskey. As the sun beat down, we said all the things the living say to the dead to erase fear and guilt. We stayed there a long time, in the punishing heat and light, until somewhere in the distance we heard a crack of thunder. Any time it rained in the desert, Mom called it a baptism. Like a plague of locusts, dark clouds crested over the mesas, extinguishing the day as the first monsoon of the season moved overhead. I held my sister's hand and we rooted our feet in the earth, holding our faces to the sky, waiting for forgiveness.

Drill

The rumor is it isn't a drill. That's always the rumor. Then the list of suspects: the loners, the bullied, the weirdos, the boys who torched anthills in grade school and slingshot quail high in middle school. Narrow down the names. Narrow down to one. Run with it. Whisper it between your thighs with your backpack overhead. Catch the flexibility of your physics partner, the one you made that catapult with in his garage, got a 1580 on his SATs, has a full scholarship to Stanford in the fall. Smell the citrus of his sweat as he insists it's only a drill. Says it three times with his eyes closed. Listen hard through the locked door for the pop-pop, the chaos. Half of you think it's a drill; half of you don't. Wonder if silence is worse. Someone is hyperventilating. Tell everyone to shut the fuck up. The teacher won't mind you swearing. Tell everyone to stay down. Listen hard. Listen harder while everyone texts words that aren't enough in a space where no one ever thought their lives were threatened—not really—into the possibility of the drill not being a drill. No announcements. Everyone is breathing hard. Everyone is holding hands.

Where the Brittlebush Bloom

Kelsey was one of the few trailer park kids riding the bus in middle school, smelling like creosote and sage, hair tangled, skin marked. She named her bruises, had stories about quad riding and cowboying. Tex, her twin brother, was teaching her to rope and ride. She wasn't going to be just another buckle bunny hanging out at the rodeos in their wide stitched jeans, silver and turquoise crosses dipping into the cleavage of their pearl-snap blouses. She wanted to bull ride or saddle bronc, though they didn't let girls do that. Girls barrel raced, or calf and team roped. The prettiest were the rodeo queens, sitting high on their horses, waving and smiling, an illusion of defiance as they leaned into their scripted roles of glitter and sash.

I told her I wanted to be a rodeo queen, but really I wanted Tex's attention. My father listened to Patsy Cline and Ian Tyson, sang songs about cowboys and loneliness, the violent and soft kind of love he felt the desert was capable of. Tex seemed to embody all of that. He had the bulk of a rodeo pick-up man, slinging cowboys over his saddle before they got gored or trampled by roughstock. He was already six foot in eighth grade, one of the tallest and strongest boys in the school, and I loved how his physical features were a sharp contrast to his soft-spoken ways; how he found a balance between labor and kindness, and sat up all night with his dog Cash, tending to her newborn pups.

For as much as I would've liked, Kelsey never invited me over, and I never asked. I knew my mother wouldn't let me. While my father loved the West and its people, my mother had spent too much of her life outside of Philadelphia and never adjusted to the change in culture. Kelsey spared us both and always came to my house and was picked up by her brother on horseback. Most of the kids on our bus lived in the same expanding developments as I did, brown tract homes on a flat stretch of Sonoran Desert, forty miles outside of Phoenix, with a wall of mountains in the distance. Kelsey got off at the last stop, the final end of blacktop with another half-mile walk into the desert.

"See that mountain, Ruby?" she pointed. "That's my backyard."

"My dad says it's state property."

"Yeah, well my daddy says the government can't tell us what to do," she said, scraping her teeth with her fingernail. "He and a few neighbors put together a roping arena for me and Tex and some of the other cowboys. I'm gonna ride bulls."

"Never saw a girl bull ride before."

"Not yet, ya haven't. Already rode a few broncs."

One Monday she declared herself free to come over. Mom wasn't too fond of Kelsey, on what I thought was account of her using the guest towels and eating all our snacks, but I knew she and Dad would be gone, watching my brother's soccer game.

After a few bowls of sugary cereal, she ran to my closet, digging through my clothes with the idea of dressing up, though I thought we were a little old for that. But when Kelsey got an idea in her head there was no stopping her. She was fearless in a way I'd never seen from a girl.

"We'll be brides together," she said, layering clothes over her jeans and t-shirt, before pulling them off. "What am I thinking?" she laughed. "Someone has to be the groom."

She ran to my brother's closet, pulled a shirt over her head then tied a flannel shirt around her thin waist. "A tuxedo tail," she said, fanning it out. Then she tucked her long dark hair into a ball cap.

She went back to my closet and found my white, satin and lace communion dress.

"Here, put this on."

It was a size too small, but I kept my arms close to my sides so it wouldn't rip.

"Now what?"

"Now we walk into the desert for marriage before someone comes for us."

"Who would come for us?" I asked, but Kelsey was already in the kitchen tearing through some snacks to bring along.

Outside the evening sun was hot and prickly as we followed a hiking trail along the foothills. It had been a wet spring and the mountains were covered in the yellow brittlebush blooms, orange Mexican poppies, and creosote budding next to their gray, fuzzy seedpods. When we got to the base of Juniper Peak, we turned in the direction of the trailer park. I was curious to see it up close thinking Kelsey would finally let me come over and I could see Tex. It was always a speck of white in the distance and a source of contention amongst the expanding gated communities, ours included. There were petitions being sent around and flyers in our mailbox about hearings on the rights of our residents, the improper and illegal use of land. But I never paid close attention.

Along the way Kelsey picked the brittlebush flowers and made me a golden bouquet to hold. She grabbed my hand and talked about how she'd join a rodeo circuit and I could tag along. We'd gotten far from my house and the burrs collecting along the hem of my dress were starting to itch, but I couldn't help notice how happy Kelsey was, nothing like the girl I knew on the bus. In fact, I couldn't even tell she was a girl. I'd never seen her looking so much like herself, not peering over her shoulder, or hanging her head low at school. I thought maybe nature had messed up and she'd been better off a boy.

"You know what would make this day even better?"

"What?" I asked, putting my nose to the bouquet of brittlebush blooms, smelling last week's rain.

"You see me ride." She swung my hand and looked up at the mountains. "It would make it perfect."

We talked more about school and the mean teachers, about what we could do to make money that involved road trips and seeing the sequoias in California. When we heard a horse and saw a rider come out of the wash, Kelsey quickly dropped my hand.

"There's the little desert rat," her brother said, looking between the two of us. "Hi, Ruby."

Before I could say hi back, Kelsey stood in front of me. "I want to show Ruby our arena."

"Come on, Kels. Maybe another time. Mom's in one of her moods. She's packing things up and talking about taking to the road again." He extended his hand out to Kelsey, leaning down from his saddle, but she shook him off.

"I'm showing Ruby our arena."

"Suit yourself," he said, then he tipped his hat to me and made me blush.

When we got there, Tex was still on his horse, riding alongside a bronc who'd just thrown a cowboy. He grabbed the rein and brought him back for the next rider.

"Good. They're still bucking out," Kelsey said. She pointed to the bull in a pen. "That's El Matón. They say if you can last eight seconds on him, you can last a lifetime anywhere. And I'm gonna ride him one day, Ruby."

It didn't look like anyone there was willing to as he kicked and thrashed at the metal fencing. I felt silly and self-conscious in my communion dress, still clutching the bouquet of flowers. I begged Kelsey not to leave me there, but she snuck off, back to her trailer to change, and came back looking like one of the cowboys, wearing chaps over her jeans and spurs on her boots. I could see her begging and arguing with Tex. Finally, she hopped up on one of the broncs in the bucking chute, leaned way back in the saddle, holding on to a thick rein before giving a nod. A cowboy lifted the chute and out she flew, one hand reaching for sky, both heels of her boots high on the horse's shoulders as he thrashed, bucking and spinning. She stayed on for a few precious seconds before being thrown. Tex, who had been hovering by her, jumped down from his saddle. He looked relieved and held out his hand. She didn't grab it so I ran over, and when her eyes found me, she slowly grinned. I handed her the bouquet of flowers just as my mother pulled up and beeped.

That night, I threw out my communion dress; and the next day, Kelsey and Tex weren't on the bus. Within a week, the trailers and the arena in the distance were gone, too. Nothing but a dusty, barren lot. Turned out the government sided with the gated communities and didn't see it fit to exist. Eviction, my mother said, when it felt more like erasure. Even the desert took over and covered the lot with blooms the following spring.

When I close my eyes, I sometimes hear the fading rattle and rage of El Matón kicking in his pen, trying to break free, with Kelsey on the ground, a halo of dirt and cowboys around her, a huge smile across her face, and the golden brittlebush blooms rising up the mountains lifting her for another ride.

Pioneer Girl

The pioneer girl suffered from melancholy. That's how they referred to her solemn ways—melancholia. Her parents decided to move out West for sunshine and dry air. Her mother always referred to West as being *out,* something in the distance, and East as going *back,* a rewinding of time.

Out West there is sunshine. Back East there are cold winters and gray days.

When they got to Missouri they followed the California Trail, averaging about ten miles a day on foot. Her father with his bad knees and her mother with her arthritis trying to keep up with the girl, whose mood seemed to improve despite the hardships. Every morning the pioneer girl would wake with her things neatly packed ready to keep moving. Her parents were relieved at her happy spirits as they walked alongside her despite their ailments, their sore bones, their dry, dusty mouths, the relentless sun turning their skin reptilian.

When will she settle? her mother whispered to the father when they hit Wyoming. Their stomachs gnawed with hunger, their eyes burned with daylight, but the pioneer girl only seemed to gather strength.

She'll settle soon, her father assured.

They tried to convince the girl after crossing two states to take up residency. The pioneer girl's father took off his socks, rubbed his blisters, wiped his brow, coughing up a darkening shadow in his lungs. But the girl's smile was infectious and so the father wrapped his feet and put each one in front of the other, propelled by their daughter's insatiable desire for more land, more light, more expanse. They climbed mountains and valleys, shed enough weight to expose every one of their fatigued bones until, at last, they stood at the edge of the Pacific Ocean where the pioneer girl's parents collapsed.

What was left to pioneer? they thought with relief.

The pioneer girl kissed their argyle skin as they sighed their final sigh, closed their eyes for the last time, satisfaction upon their face. Then she set out into the water, kicking her legs, paddling her arms toward the sun squeezed between sea and sky, into the softening blue. Upon the final swallow of light, she turned to float on her back, weightless at last—nothing in front of her, nothing behind. Nothing but a canvas of her own making.

Saguaro

An ancient rain sticks to creosote and sage the way my memory clings to childhood the way your ashes adorn these peaks circled by hawks the way a single saguaro braves the altitude two arms stretched out like a cross a hug a headstone the way an August monsoon slices the baked summer sky and water is held in a century of limbs the way you lay on your deathbed and asked when are you coming home and I said soon because words felt like wind and wind felt like nothing and all I ever wanted was to please you.

Sabrina Hicks

Liquid Gold

The land stretched out around us as we combed the flats searching for a new well, said the water rights were worth more than the cattle it took to carve a path through the scrub oak and manzanitas, the cat claw that would tear a hole in your pants without a pair of chaps. We'd hop off our horses, hobble them under a juniper tree, their hooves crunching on a thick blanket of berries, sharpening the air with the gin we'd drink later in the evenings. We'd look for a good branch, one that looked like a Y, hold the handlebar sides and walk in circles.

When the stem pulls down, we hit water, you said. *This is how the ancients did it. Witching.*

When we weren't looking for water we were looking for arrowheads, for Manos and matates, stones long ago tribes used for grinding corn. We'd look for tracks and scat. Signs of life that used to exist before a long drought pushed them to distant valleys. *We are always standing on a story.*

We walked for hours with the wind freezing our ears, agitating our horses, trying to pretend we could leave behind the modern world, that all we needed was a stick to find what you called liquid gold, that the land would provide, would rise again from the ashes the way the city of Phoenix did after the ancient tribe of Hohokam left, leaving behind the ruins of their Salt River Valley irrigation, that there was a pulse of a river below us if we only listened. You were convinced we had the same instincts as the tribes from long ago. But our instincts were too muddled by encroachment, by the noise of growth and our modern toys, the quads tearing through brush, the planes overhead with their trails of exhaust, further removing us from the land, from ourselves.

We never did see liquid gold—only felt it as we wandered the high desert with our sticks, talking about the weather, how long the drought would last, when we thought the next storm would come and fill the tanks for the cattle. We'd open our canteens and quench our dry mouths, talking about water and rain, the love language of desert dwellers, two dreamers standing on the dry earth packed with secrets, covered in dust waiting for the skies to open and soften the land. With thunderclouds overhead, our sticks pulled down and our chests swelled with hope.

We scattered your ashes on a high mountain overlooking the flats, the canyons, the twin buttes, carved your name into a rock pitched high enough to see for miles, and I wonder sometimes if you're riding that wave of liquid gold, just waiting for us to join you. You never did like riding out alone.

Sabrina Hicks

Pick-Me-Girl

When the good old boys started disappearing, everyone went to the pick-me-girl to find out what she knew, though not telling was part of the code—no narcs, no spilling secrets, everything delivered should be done so brutally, especially honesty. And never trust anything that doesn't sting.

The search parties combed the forest with dogs while the pick-me-girl watched from behind the trees.

I can drink you all under the table, she said when she joined the campfire of men.

Never seen a girl pack them away like that.

They told her to smile and she did. They told her to lose weight and she strived for a thin disappearance. They told her to keep quiet and she silenced herself with cleaning. They asked her how to get girls and she told them where to move, where to touch. *Practice on me,* she said, as they murmured their love for her in her ear, their bodies hard against hers, pressing in a way that almost convinced her it was enough to hold their vulnerabilities in the dark.

They didn't know she'd spent her childhood under the spit and rage of men, accustomed to the red ripened skin of violence peeling away from its flesh like the tomatoes her mother boiled in an effort to please the appetites of men. So many boyfriends, step-fathers, brothers and step-brothers, and her—pick-me-girl—chosen to diffuse their hair-triggered temperaments, set off by a misplaced pack of smokes, a dirty sink, empty fridge, a football loss, money clips short of a bill, and the aching disappointment that life tucked in their joints, raised to believe the world was theirs for the picking. Pick-me-girl ducked and weaved her way through the bramble of violence, shrinking herself into landscape. She told herself to blend, enter at the right moment. Timing is everything.

She kept track of her missteps, when she failed and ended up with a busted lip, a bruised rib or eye, logging each one in a tiny book until there was no place left to store what her bones could no longer handle. Her timing had been off as of late. More and more she found herself alone, wandering the woods, following the bloom of moss-covered trees, and the deer slipping undetected along the dissecting brooks. She'd watch the slick mirrored sky stretch clouds until they broke, a piece made whole upon its breakage. She felt the spongy ground lead and slope to a ring of rocks circling a hidden well, endless black spiraling into a pupil, and she knew she found the eye of the forest. A place where the brutality of nature, muted and underestimated, cloaked in beauty, rich in oxygen, is both muse and warden. There wouldn't be a trace of her leading them there, picking them off one by one for the fall. How the birds sang sweetly over their cries. How the clouds darkened the ground for the swallow, and the trees, accustomed to the swift blade of an axe, shook their leaves. And the girl, handpicked, chosen at last.

Sabrina Hicks

Rattlesnakes

I need to set the record straight—I'm no killer. Arsonist or thief is fair. But killer ain't. Though to be honest, I've been known to dance on a grave or two on account of who's doing the dying. But right hand to God, Cyrus was the one who came up with the suicide pact. He just assumed I'd follow on account of his inflated sense of himself.

The debt and bankruptcy—that's on him. I wasn't gonna off myself because of his delinquencies. Any woman worth her salt knows you can fix a man's haircut but you can't fix his soul. His addictions got us into that mess, the worst of 'em being the gambling. He said there was no sense in being a spectator without having some skin in the game. Problem was he was skin-deep in grift since the day he was born. Mama always said crazy don't show itself for at least a few months, but Cyrus maintained a false sense of sanity for a year. He was the kind of liar who believed his own lies, which is a level of deception that's harder to root out.

It'd been a particularly rough week of creditors, collectors, a hitman with a heart, who gave him one more day to come up with a sum neither of 'em would see, and a foreclosure notice on the little house his daddy left him, when he decided it was game over. Then he made a case for shootin' ourselves like we was Romeo and Juliet. But it wasn't like we were married. I'd only been running with him just over a year.

"Darlin'," I offered, "how 'bout I use my gun, you use yours, and we count to three? That way the blood stays on our own hands. Heaven being heaven an' all. More of an argument at the pearly gates. Though I'm fairly certain there's a verse in the good book frownin' on any part of this."

"Clementine, you gotta point."

Now depending on how much time you spent roped around the bible belt, you wouldn't believe, but that man considered himself a man of God.

"And if you go first, babe, I'll pray for your soul," I said.

He nodded. "You're a good woman."

I nodded back, knowing I had no intention of doing such a thing and no intention of joining his ass. Though I felt twice my age, I'd only spent eighteen years on this earth, all under the thumb of someone else, and I'd finally reached the age of independence. Cyrus on the other hand had at least ten years on me, though he was cagey about his exact age. He was never good at countin', let alone reading women. He killed himself on four.

We sat in his pink bathtub, me in between his legs like spoons staring at the moldy grout because he didn't wanna leave a mess for his sister who'd be the first to come by. Awfully gracious of him if you ask me. When I heard his gun go off I lowered mine and took a long, deep breath. I didn't look back but he never said, *Hey babe, you're supposed to fire, too,* so I assumed he was good and dead. I sat there frozen, feeling the heat of his blood run down my back and around my legs like I was filling up a warm bath.

For some reason it seemed like I'd given birth sitting there in all that blood. I got on a bit of a laughing kick, which makes me sound like a real lunatic but you have to understand, when I get into uncomfortable situations, my wiring is off. I did all my cryin' before Mama died and then that salty spicket inside me got swapped out for laughter. My foster daddy said I was a well run dry with only rattlesnakes at the bottom. I lost Mama at eleven, never had a Pa, and was thrown into the state of Wyoming's foster care system where I slept with a switchblade I traded for things I'm ashamed to say now. But when you sleep with one eye open, it's always better knowing you can gut a pig when you find one squealing on top of you. Bein' sweet was never a luxury I could afford.

I'm not sure how long I sat there in that warm bath. I leaned back into Cy's chest, wrapped his thick arms around me and felt a calm that almost felt like love, like I was drownin' in rose petals, though I know love is the wrong word. More like comin' up for air in a lake of weeds and undertow. When I finally came around, I showered and got to work cleanin'. I knew Cyrus had a garage full of diesel and turpentine. His body reeked of the stuff from working on his old truck. I told him, if I lit my cigarettes too close he'd burst into flames.

Didn't take much to burn that tinderbox. I didn't think how it might look to the cops until I was out of Afton heading to Dally's in Smoot. I wasn't so good at thinkin' ahead, but I figured forensics would see the man took his own life like in them cop shows. Only the fire was my idea at that point. Growin' up we had burn barrels. No sanitation workers came to the farm. Can't fault a woman for good housekeeping.

At first, Dally wasn't too keen on me showing up, but I needed some money and company.

"Clementine, you're about to become a fugitive."

"Been everything else," I said. "May as well be that."

"Yeah, but you're about to make me an accomplice."

"Dally, that man you got in that trailer ain't no better than the one I hitched my wagon to. And even then, I'd argue mine was a hell of a lot better."

"Kyle's at work right now," she said, as if she was arguing details.

To be honest, I knew it wouldn't take much to convince her to leave. Dally had a pregnancy that took a few months ago before Kyle knocked her on her ass and she miscarried. She was what the guys called a looker so I wasn't sure why she thought Kyle was the best life had to offer. Maybe it'd be easier if we got a choice of parents and childhoods. Dally was another foster kid in a broke town, which meant folks that got her needed the state check way more than they needed another mouth to feed. Meanest bunch of church-goers I'd ever seen, so I couldn't be too hard on Dally for her choices.

"You know Thelma and Louise?"

"The movie?" she said, one hand on her skinny waist, finally coming off the stoop of her trailer. "Yeah, I've seen it."

"Well, you can be Thelma and I'll be Louise. Or if you want, you be Louise and I'll be Thelma cause I can't remember which one was which and neither of us has red hair."

"You know they both died."

I looked at the encroachment of brush around the falling apart trailer, the 100-foot patch of dirt with a firepit at the center and beer cans littering the yard like lawn trolls.

"Darlin', we're all dying," I said. "Just a matter of timing. Hell, I almost died today. There was a good chance Cyrus would've changed the plan and shot me first."

She couldn't argue with that logic.

"Clementine and Dally. Dally and Clementine," she said, trying out titles while looking up at the sky. It was June in Wyoming. Warm and balmy and smelling of Rocky Mountain juniper. She spoke to the thin clouds, "Doesn't have the same ring."

"You're goddamn right it does! Got even a better ring. You listen here, Dally. You got two choices. You can either walk back in there and wait for Kyle to drink himself into a blind rage and treat you like a rag doll, or you can walk out on his ass before he puts his vile seed in you again and got a hold of you for the remainder of that kid's life, if he don't kill you first. These hick towns ain't no place for a woman needing options! I'm heading to Phoenix, crashing at my cousin's until I figure things out. She'll take you in too. She rescues animals all the time. Couple of strays like us can't be any different."

That seemed to shake her up, so I thought I'd strike. "How much cash you got?"

A slow smile slid across her face. "Kyle's got a secret stash somewhere in case of emergencies."

I grinned back at her. She was warming up to the idea faster than I'd predicted.

"Well, I say this is an emergency."

I followed her into the trailer and we scoured the place, looking behind every shit stained cushion and questionable lump of laundry until I started thinking like that bastard. Few things I knew about Kyle: he liked to drink, he liked to slap around the ladies, and he sure did like his TV shows.

"You got any loose floorboards or soft spots in the plywood? Those Hollywood scripts always have their characters squirreling away cash in carpentry."

Sure enough it was behind the toilet in the wall. "Not a stretch for a man who likes to sit on the can," I said. Dally was really onboard when she saw that wad of cash, coming up with a list of dumb shit he did that week, thinking of the places she never saw, or the things she never did. She was kneeling beside me, counting twenties on the piss stained linoleum. Man, his aim was bad. I held my nose trying to figure how far we'd get with 520 dollars.

"Pretty good for that cheap bastard. If Cy came across this stash, he wouldn't even make it to the front door without placing a bet on how many squares left on your toilet paper roll."

"I feel like we should go to Mexico," she said.

"Nah, that's suspect. Everyone knows you only go to Mexico when you kill someone."

She gave me a look like she didn't believe I didn't kill Cyrus. I sighed and said, "Now why would I kill a man who had death stalking his every move? I'm no fool. Was only a matter of time."

"Okay, but if we're doing this we gotta go to the Grand Canyon like Thelma and Louise. Not to die or nothing. Just I've never seen it and I've always wanted to go and Kyle never took me."

"Then, Dally, that's where we're going," I said. "It's around ten hours to northern Arizona. We check out the canyon, then head down to Phoenix, which is another four hours. I'll drive, you DJ, but it has to be old tunes. I can't stomach what passes for country these days."

We hit the 89 South after putting together bags of food, water, and clothing. Somewhere behind us was the smoke from the fire I'd started and it was only a matter of time before someone came looking for Cy's truck. We drove the border of Idaho before hitting

Utah when I started to believe I'd thrown Dally a lifeline the way she was comin' up with ideas of where we oughta go. She'd had all sorts of dreams stashed inside her that came spilling out on the highway. I told her with a face like hers, she should take her chances in LA, though even as I said it I realized I sounded like Cyrus, suggesting fanciful ideas. I was fairly certain Hollywood was crowded with pretty faced girls ditching their small town roots.

I wasn't interested in the bright lights so I didn't quite know. But it made Dally into a new woman and I liked seeing her giddy with options. We stopped for gas and littered the cab with corn nuts, beef jerky, Bazooka bubblegum (her choice), Big Hunks (mine), and Red Bull to stay awake. We peeled off twenties from Kyle's wad of cash cackling like two schoolgirls, singing along to June Carter and Johnny Cash. I was feeling right as rain having Dally beside me.

"Nothing like driving an open highway to feel the rush of possibilities," I said, chewing on my Big Hunk.

"What do you think Kyle's doing right now?"

"Don't know. Don't care." I looked over at Dally for a gut check. "Don't be thinking about him. Time you thought about yourself. When's the last time you did that?"

Apparently, Dally wasn't a dry well like me. She started crying.

I put my hand on her shoulder. "There's no worse a man out there than one who raises his hand to a woman. No part of you should grieve for that lowlife or think you was responsible. It's a cancer of what I call the little man and it only grows back if you think you can carve it out."

She nodded and wiped her eyes. It was nighttime and the highway shrunk to our cast of headlights. Traffic was light and the mood changed as it does in evening. Maybe we were coming off our sugar high, but I felt we were outrunning some consequences that were gaining speed, and I kept checking the rearview mirror. It seemed, too, Dally needed some reassurances which required an amount of softening I wasn't accustomed to.

"It's hard to see now in the dark, but we're almost there," I said. "And around us, Dally, this land we're pushing through has stories, but we're the ones holding the script. That's what the open road provides. Livin' on our own terms!"

We hit the Grand Canyon late at night and slept in the car. When the sun rose, we saw the red rock light up and deepen into the canyon and we got out to walk the rim. Now, I know everyone says the Grand Canyon can't be captured in photos and paintings, and maybe even words, but what I saw I wasn't prepared for. It's like a secret pact happens between your heart and your eyes, opening something so deep inside you, you didn't know it was there in the first place. Dally was hiking down to a lower spot off the road, toward a ledge that gave a panoramic view, and I slowly followed her taking in the vastness of the land. Each layer of sediment ran like rivers in the canyon wall, veins of all the sunrises and sunsets that happened in the West—ones never captured or maybe even seen except for in those pages of rock.

Deep below us was the Colorado River running aqua colored and jagged like a scar. I sat next to Dally watching the sun shape the mesas, shifting the rock sculptures, dotting the landscape. There were trees growing in the damnedest places, too, leaning out from the edges, roots prying through stone and spilling out like entrails. The wind gave them enough movement to look like they were risking it all being that close. That they believed their leaves were wings if only their roots would give. We sat there a good long time before Dally broke the silence.

"We're just a couple of rattlesnakes," Dally said, hugging her knees.

Maybe for the first time since we left, I looked at Dally. She'd be easy to dismiss as just another pretty face, but faces are deceitful. She closed her eyes and laid back with her hands behind her head.

"Rattlesnakes are just out there minding their own business, not trying to hurt no one, finding food to eat and rocks to sun on," she said. "They even rattle a warning or two, but some people think snakes should die just for being snakes, for being who they are. When, really, they just want to go on living, same as you and me, only striking cause they've been pushed too far. You know they sense things before anyone else?"

I lay next to Dally in the crook of her arm the way I used to with Mama before she got in that vehicle and crashed on the interstate. I was in sixth grade, Ms. Sawyer's class, when I was told to go to the office. I remember the smell of paint on my fingers. I kept trying to rub the colors off when I got the news. The principal was waiting for me to cry, but I didn't. I couldn't imagine her not coming home. I couldn't imagine a world I wanted to live in without her, so I didn't. Crying meant she was gone.

Dally pulled me in tight and rested her cheek on my head. "You know what I mean, Clemie? 'Bout rattlesnakes? Kyle killed one the other day. Wasn't anywhere near our trailer. It was moving along the brush, but Kyle couldn't let it go. Kept saying it would be back as if it was vengeful. He stalked it with a shovel and smashed its head until you couldn't tell it was anything but a stain in dirt. I was so mad I cried. I cried and couldn't stop. Got Kyle so angry. He accused me of caring more about that old snake than losing our baby."

I brushed away Dally's hair blowing in my face, feeling something grow inside me.

"The thing is, he was right. I never shed a tear over that miscarriage. What does that make me?"

"Makes you human," I said, feeling that something inside me rise to my skin and dislodge in my chest. Dally must've felt it too. She gripped me even tighter, holding on to me like she was the roots and I was one of those trees on the edge. "I believe that snake was trying to warn you, Dally."

Maybe it was all that beauty, open and exposed. The land flat on each side until you stumble upon this secret so massive in scale it seems unreal. But it's real. It was there before us and it would be there after. Only thing brief was our silly lives. I began crying being around so much beauty, like that paint on my hands had never come off until then, sliding down my fingertips, bleeding into river and rock, into dawn and dusk. Because there was joy in that cry too, and maybe that's what hurt the most, the fact that I dared to still care about something that held no shape until that moment. Maybe I was even crying for Cyrus, who'd never see what the world was capable of, for the moments in bed lying next to him when he was just a boy with dreams too big for his body. And when the cops came and called down to me and Dally, we didn't move. We lay there holding on to one another. We didn't launch ourselves off the cliff like in the movies. We weren't Thelma and Louise. We were Dally and Clementine. Clementine and Dally.

Olympus Mons

Lucy sits in her backyard with a ring of dirt around her, cup of water, red paint rocks between her legs as she drags her fingers across her cheeks. Two stripes under each eye like a warrior.

"What are you doing, Loser?" her brother says, kicking a stone in her direction, hitting her knee. He's on his way to his friend's house and she breathes a sigh of relief.

"Going home," Lucy says. "To the red planet. I'm a Martian. I don't belong here." But she says it quiet, in her own language to keep her safe. If he understood, he'd erupt like the volcanos back home, liquid orange, drying into burnt copper. She looks up at the marble sky, threads of clouds snagging, knows there will be rain.

"I need more aluminum foil," Lucy says to her mom, but her mom is sitting at a table with so much paperwork around her that her worn expression feels like a black hole, one she is scared of getting sucked into. She starts to feel the gravitational pull, the inevitable crush, and backs away, walking the way astronauts do, so little gravity keeping her down. She walks that way at school, placing one foot in front of the other like Neil and Buzz, only lighter because she's a girl, she doesn't leave footprints, she knows how to be a shadow. She doesn't make a sound at night when she creeps outside to see the moon, to watch it rest on the branches where she slingshots stars across the galaxy. She sings campfire songs to Venus, the one about the big rock candy mountains, where there's lemonade springs, lakes of stew, her stomach is never empty, and she doesn't have to change her socks.

The foil in the drawer is from the Dollar Store, the cheap off-brand one that balls into nothing. She hoards pebbles of tin along with the red rocks—a reminder of her return. The foil has good conductivity, it's malleable, it can bend into antennas, it doesn't look of this world. On some days, she even thinks it's enough to get her back to the red planet. She dreams about the rover collecting samples, about how Olympus Mons is the largest volcano in our solar system, over two and a half times the height of Mount Everest and nearly as wide as Arizona. She dreams about that view on Mars, her lungs taking in the thin air, jumping three times higher, how there are lakes of red bean stew in the cavities of that candy mountain—no hunger, sweets every day.

When Lucy signs up for the fourth-grade science fair she tells the teacher the rover on Mars doesn't know where to get the best samples. That she can give the scientists everything they need to study her planet. They're looking for life in all the wrong places. They have to dig below the surface. She imagines the roots of trees, the unseen web of communications in an underworld. The teacher musses up her stringy sun-soaked hair, releasing its earthy smell, and Lucy knows the teacher doesn't understand. She holds the stink of a dying star.

"Hey, Loser," her brother says in between bites of his Swanson dinner he threw in the oven for both of them. Her mother is away again and won't be home for days. There's a few cans of beans in the pantry, bread and beer in the refrigerator. "There is no life on Mars for a reason. You'd fry up with radiation. You remember Arnold Schwarzenegger's face melting in Total Recall?" He stretches the skin by his ears until his eyes bulge and his teeth chatter like a skeleton, bits of gravy spilling from his mouth.

On the day of the science fair, Lucy stands by her project covered in red dust, her rover made of aluminum foil, waiting to explain how it works, wanting to tell anyone who will listen that she should be on a mission to Mars. Earthlings can't handle that kind of solitude but she can. She was born into a great silence. She knows the language of wind and soil, how invisibility works, how something molten can harden into rock. She waits for the judges to make their way to her, after they're done hovering around projects constructed with Styrofoam balls, painted into perfect miniature planets, projects that help them understand all the ways they have failed as a species, polluting its air and waterways, altering temperatures. Projects that, after given their good marks, will end up in a landfill waiting their thousand-year decomposition and the kids will sit that evening with ice cream and praise. She overhears an explanation of charts and graphs as she waits her turn, resisting the gravity trying to hold her back, humming to her big rock candy mountain, two stripes under each eye like a warrior.

Sabrina Hicks

Scar Tissue

The night we played twenty-one questions, you asked me to tell you something real about myself, then laughed and said, *even though you have no heart*. It only occurred to me later, after I sent you home, you were being playful. I'm sorry I assumed the worst, that I'm always ready for battle, that I grew up on Bruce Lee and Jet Li movies, craving justice and revenge. What I couldn't tell you is that I spent too many nights on my childhood bed staring up at the popcorn ceiling, longing to bend the shapes that crept along styrofoam valleys and peaks, crack a spine with nunchucks and hear the splinter of relief. And then, how do I say this after being told I have no heart? I never want to affirm anyone's belief in me, regardless of assertion or accuracy. I cannot unravel before you. You are not prepared for that. I am not prepared for that. I once had a large scrape on my elbow that wouldn't heal. My mother, before leaving, told me to stop picking at it, told me I would let the demons in if I continued; the scab is the heal, the gate that keeps them out. But I did. Every night. Pick, pick, pick. My navy sheets hid the blood stains as she kissed me for the last time, told me to behave for my father. Be a man. I was nine. I blamed the open wound. I blamed the shadow crawl. I blamed my fragile, gaping heart.

My Drugstore Queen

Maeve walks the CVS aisles high as those Mylar balloons, the ones that break free from their cage or slip loose from a hand, trapped in corners of tall ceilings. She tears the plastic seals off tubes of lipsticks and compacts of iridescent eyeshadows, coloring her face like the wings of a still hummingbird as I run down the aisles after her, inhaling pine and lemon, Skittles and holiday chocolates, skimming the Hallmark cards celebrating lifetime achievements she'll never see: graduations, marriages, births, anniversaries. The pharmacist yells over the counter, *Girls, you have to pay for that now.* Maeve inspects her newly painted nails she finished in aisle 5b, Alley Cat black, pouts her Jolly Rancher red lips, tugs down her sun-faded top and whispers in his ear with her warm watermelon breath words that throw him back to middle school and hard-ons. We're both thirteen, but no one ever thinks Maeve is thirteen. Not ever. She turns her head, sticks out her candy-coated tongue. We have the place now. Outside the rain hits sideways and somewhere Maeve's mother is finishing her shift at Waffle House and will walk across the street to the trucker bar, tend to the drunks and bring one home; somewhere my mother is cooking dinner and will wait for me, looking at the clock, meatloaf growing cold while my father watches football. And all I smell is sun and possibilities when Maeve peels off the seals of scented lotions: coconuts, Hawaii, waves. *Do you smell the beach?* she inhales, closing her eyes long enough to feel she is slipping away into a riptide. She grabs hair dye. *We become blonds and get the fuck out of here.* And I nod, thinking I'd follow her anywhere. Maeve, the only girl who'd talk to me in eighth grade. Maeve, the girl my father called white trash. *We get the fuck out of here,* I repeat. Maeve, the girl who will go missing in two years and never be found, looking like a stained-glass saint under these fluorescent lights.

Sabrina Hicks

Rock Collection

The first rock struck me in the head after a neighbor boy told me to go to hell. I can't remember why, only that he had blond hair and a vicious smile, smelled like the boys at recess with their peanut butter fingers pulling at the training bras worn by girls like me, impatient to become a woman they could imagine posing in a magazine. I pocketed the rock to feel the weight of hell. It stayed in my backpack for years, whittled down by the edges of childhood.

The second was in high school, kissing a boy on a soft patch of grass under an olive tree. A rock pinched under the weight of us pressed together. I dislodged it from my backside, cursing before slipping it into my pocket, shifting my body onto a bed of stones, sinking into the hard points. The boy followed me. *Better?* he asked, his face unsure in the moonlight before he swallowed what I knew to be true: *A lone nail will impale you, but a bed can be laid upon*. The kissing boy was my first taste of gravity.

The third rock presented like an anchor, a gift from a college boy who had slipped in and out of my room, my classes, my mind. He had nice teeth, the kind that saw a dentist every six months and remembered to floss. He was as beautiful as a calm sea, placid and vast. And so, I had a rock in each pocket and a rock I would twist on my finger and leave in a bowl at the end of the day so I could remember how it felt to be weightless.

A flood of rocks came after, turning my limbs to stones, my feet to concrete. My hips widened to make room. My hands grew, too. I became a monument, worshipped, public, exposed until I blended into mountains and no one saw me at all—just a woman with her pockets full of rocks. No one had to tell me that if I walked into the ocean I would sink. I just knew this to be true. And so, I became a woman on the shore, staring into a stitch of blue.

From my seaside window, I see people pointing at the tall mounds of stones I have emptied from my pockets over the years, calcifications I've shed to walk upon this earth. The cairns on my front yard, a nest of angles, reach up and up and up. Women stop and stare, nudging their husbands and lovers, their sons and brothers. *See there!* they say, their eyes climbing each rock until all they see is someone they could imagine, a woman no longer on the shore.

Sabrina Hicks

Buying Raindrops

I call a number that gets me a person on the line whose voice will ask me questions and quiet the house around me. *I'll have product 29485,* I say, looking at the raindrops midair, smile wrapped around a girl's face held up to a sun only she can see. She is hugging something, a prop to this happiness, and the woman on the line tells me I've made a great choice and I think, *I'm a person making a great choice,* and I keep her on the line with: *How durable is it? How do I take care of it? Does it come with a warranty?* She is patient and kind, says, *those are great questions,* and I think, *I'm a person asking great questions.* The empty house moans, tries to remind me of what I am not, but I'm only hearing my great questions. I pull out my credit card and read the number over the phone, misreading two digits, asking if she can hold on, and I think, *someone is waiting for me, I am a person worth waiting for.* That minute stretches and I hear frustration in her breath so I apologize because I've let it get too far, I'm losing that feeling I'm paying for and I wonder if I should hang up, but I can't because she might turn to someone next to her and say quietly she was speaking with a real weirdo, someone who wasn't worth her time. I start to forget what I'm buying until I see the raindrops midair and the smile on that beautiful little girl's face and I think, *oh yes,* and I get the numbers correct this time. I read them aloud and when she repeats them back to me I say, *yes, yes, very good,* because maybe she needs something positive too. Maybe she's having a terrible day and this makes her think she's done something very good by reading the numbers back to me correctly. Sometimes all we can ask for is a small miracle of a well-received performance. And I give her my address and the house moans so I put my hand over the receiver and say, *Hush up you!* and she asks if I have kids and then says, *Of course you do,* because of product 29485, which is generous of her when I know she wanted to say grandkids but then thought better of it, which means she's very polite and I want to tell her she was raised well, not by parents who have no time to parent, the kind found on planes, in the aisles of stores, ones who can't bother with phone calls or visits. So, I say, *I do*. I say, *They're beautiful just loud. The kind of beauty that doesn't last though or forgive,* and I allow myself a look at the framed photos of people I remember from long ago who mail me packages twice a year, Christmas and my birthday, adding to the unopened boxes in the garage, piling higher and higher, suffocating the space where my car used to be, spilling into each spare room until they are claimed. She says she understands but I hear something shift in her voice the way I do every evening with Peter, the delivery man, who used to be Mike and before him a large woman named Jeannie who smelled like peppermint and Dial soap, so I tell her she has a lovely voice because she does. It slips into each syllable like silk, like maybe she is somewhere in the South and before I can ask where she is from because I want to imagine I'm with her on a front porch sipping lemonade, smelling jasmine, gossiping about neighbors, she ends with it was so nice to talk to me and my order should be 5-7 business days and I should have a wonderful evening. And I have. I've had a wonderful evening tasting those raindrops.

Sabrina Hicks

Writing Prompts and Changing Views

At a time when real life is crushed into an acronym, IRL, to accommodate social media, texts, curated accounts, all I crave is something real, someone to talk to, my father's voice, my mother's strength. Dani was annoyed that her father sent her a text asking how she was doing, as if the weight of their collective damage could be written with thumbs. Knowing he won't answer your phone call, you text back *fine,* not explaining how you got fired for taking too many days off, caring for a woman he once loved.

A strong memory of color. I'm driving to the hospital to visit my mother with Hey Jude playing on the radio so that when I enter the lobby of broken people my head is filled with begging: *Jude, don't be afraid, Jude, don't let me down, Jude, take a sad song and make it better,* and I think for a second I'll let her into my heart so it can beat for two, like all those years before, but I don't go to her. Instead, I pretend I'm there to see someone else. I say to the front desk, *Maternity ward, please. My sister just gave birth.* And somehow, I end up staring at babies fresh from the womb, bound in white hospital blankets, striped pink and blue and yellow, brushstrokes of blood and cream-colored mucus still streaked across their brow, and I wonder what it's like to be that new, to open my eyes and see the world for the first time, to recognize my mother through static. I blink in the rich colors of life, until I'm kicked out and treated like a baby thief, like death visiting.

A time of anger or fear. She sits up, tubes scattered about, says, *Dani, don't be angry*. But Dani cannot help herself. She vacillates between sympathy and disgust, looking at the slices across her mother's veins, the dissection of life and death like the tree that fell on the roof of Dani's childhood home, nearly missing her, her mother and father on one side, she on the other, and how her mother's voice was a bridge cutting through wind and rain. Her friends console her, tell her she's stronger than her mother, implying her mother is fragile and weak, not made for this world, but she doesn't believe any of those words or explanations, only that some things cannot be explained, which is to say, everything human.

A ladybug crawls across your chest . . . Its wings, tucked underneath its brightly dotted shell, spill out, like her shirt you brought from home, coming through the zipper of her pants as you and the nurse get her dressed, before she is released from the hospital with a stack of papers on suicide prevention, group therapy, interventions, substance abuse hotlines, and bills to add to the bills you haven't paid. She will not let you fuss over her anymore she says, but the shirt coming out of her front zipper is a bookmark you save for later when your eyes are heavy, humming Hey Jude, coming undone, the speckled night crawling across your chest.

A man asleep in a car. Make it funny! Make it scary! But all you see is a reckoning, a knife placed squarely in his chest and the taste of blood waking inside you. You write about the twist. You write about your father leaving you both, leaving you caretaker, littering your childhood with each curve of road. You rip it all up and write fantasy, a Lord of the Rings knockoff where you are the hero, your father is the villain, and your mother the damsel to be saved. But how do you save someone from themself? You forget about salvation, make the car drive off a cliff, a man asleep at the wheel, a daughter looking over the edge, a mother who becomes her own hero.

A time when you were desperate or diseased.

A time when you were grateful and knew love.

A time when all the triggers buried in your chest did not require a key.

Sabrina Hicks

Extraterrestre

When I was eight, I found a dying man in my tree fort behind my house.

We lived twenty miles from the Arizona-Mexico border with nothing but desert and mountains to the south of us. My father had warned me about illegal aliens, which I assumed were the green Martians I saw on TV. It didn't occur to me that the man would be anyone other than a human being wandering the desert without food and water.

My tree fort was an overgrown paloverde with green branches tangled and weighted in mistletoe. Inside, I kept a pile of books and two old couch cushions. When I found the dying man, he was covered in dust, laying on his side with his head resting on a cushion, foaming at the mouth. We spent a good long minute staring at each other in shock, accessing our fears. But I saw more fear in him than I'd ever seen in a man, and all I wanted was to keep him safe, which I knew meant not telling anyone. My father was prone to fits of rage, and my mother took pills, patting the side of her head like something had come loose.

I was happy to have a secret, to care for someone who made me feel seen and needed. I brought him water and crackers and an endless supply of leftover meatloaf my mother made twice weekly, which no one seemed to like except for the dying man. He nodded to me, saying *gracias*, which was the only Spanish word I knew. Each day he seemed to be getting better and stronger; each day he taught me a new word: *ojos, boca, corazón*.

I brought him comics with silly pictures and a stuffed bear he called Oso. *Como estas y Oso?* I learned to say as I greeted him, coming directly from the bus stop after school. He smiled and laughed and patted the dirt for me to sit. *La escuela es muy importante*, he said. I nodded in agreement because I loved third grade. I loved my teacher, Mrs. Stanwick. More than anything, I loved not being home. I did my homework while he stared up through the treetop humming songs I didn't know but made me think of flowers growing on a vine in a faraway place. Sometimes he'd sing to a creased photo of a woman and children he kept in his back pocket. *Your family?* I asked. *Si,* he nodded. *Mi familia.*

It sounded so beautiful rolling off his tongue, the way quail calls its young, and I smiled, thinking I could be part of his family too. I pointed to my house and said, *Mi familia.* He nodded but looked concerned, and for a moment we shared a new secret, one I'd been keeping even from myself, that my father yelled at my mother about things she wasn't doing right, that I'd stick to the scant shadows of the desert for as long as possible to avoid his belt, that my family was broken.

Pablo, he said, patting his chest. *Jennifer,* I said, patting my head. He pointed to my heart and said, *Ángel.* And I beamed with pride because I knew that word.

At dinner, my father spoke about things I didn't understand, about no good politicians, taxation, aliens who came to sell drugs and take our jobs, reminding me of that movie I'd seen between my fingers at my cousin's house where space invaders took over human bodies. I began to wonder if it had happened to him; his face shifting into an angry mask as the night wore on. I had remembered a happier version of him, a time when his breath wasn't sour and his tongue wasn't sharp.

I thought I should warn Pablo about these body snatchers when I took him leftovers that night, not wanting him to turn into someone his family wouldn't recognize. I looked up *alien* in the English-Spanish translation book I'd borrowed from school. *Extraterrestre.* Then I gathered a plate of leftovers and a new jug of water. I was almost to my fort when I heard my father behind me.

"What the hell are you doing?" he asked, propping himself up on our cinderblock wall. He'd been laying down, looking up at the night sky.

"Nothing," I said.

"Why're you carrying a plate of meatloaf?"

I was good at lying at that point, keeping his moods at bay, but I stood with the plate shaking in one hand and a jug of water sloshing around in the other.

"Thought I'd have dinner in my fort," I said.

The full moon shone upon his face in a silver haze, gutting his eyes, lighting up the amber bottle clutched in his fist.

"We just ate. And you hate your ma's meatloaf."

The blood flowing in my body began to burn as he hopped off the wall and walked toward me. His eyes followed mine to my fort.

"You have someone in there?" Dad walked over to the tree, ripped the branches apart and disappeared inside.

"Pablo!" I yelled, dropping the food and water, rushing in behind him. Dad spun around in the empty space.

"Pablo?" he said, then repeated it as he shoved me to the ground. "If I ever find a boy in here, I'll kill 'em."

I looked up at him, an ink mark looming above me, his face a distortion of shadows and shapes. As he left, the moon took his place, shining through the broken branches to the spot where Oso laid, and scrawled deep in the dirt next to him was a drawing of an angel with the name *Jennifer* scrawled underneath.

Dead Animal Pick Up

In the beam of headlights, we found the massive heap on the shoulder of the highway, a half-dead bull elk pawing up at the moon, eyes like river stones and a rack that could gouge holes in the porous, starlit sky.

Shoot, Papa said, coming to a stop. *He's still alive, and I left my shotgun at home. Mayberry, stay here while I go back.* He rolled down the window as I got out. *And keep away from his horns or he'll impale you.*

At twelve, I'd never been left alone before on a call. Usually the smell of death was thick in the air by the time we got there. But the cool morning ripened the juniper and sage, and the grass shone with mist rolling off the mountains, hovering above the trees like ghosts, the stretch of road dripping in the ink of pre-dawn light.

Papa would say it was their time, as if the remote forest highway pulsing with semis, sport utility vehicles and Mack trucks was a liminal threshold determining an animal's fate. I saw it in their eyes, time taking them by surprise, and I wondered if time allowed them one last look at the infinite blue, the passing of clouds, the tiny moments that become extraordinary through the lens of death.

I buried my hands deep in my coat pockets, fighting off a chill, while the elk began moaning a high-pitched wail across the highway, into the slope of aspens and Rocky Mountain junipers. I tried not thinking about it suffering like Mama had before she died last year, or that maybe it was calling for its own mother in the distance. I took small steps testing his reaction, crouching to my knees with my hands held out, not caring about the trouble I'd be in if he got a burst of energy and whipped his head around. The bull lifted his neck at my approach, rested back on the grass, his eyes growing heavy, his breath calming as I laid my hand on his underside, away from where he'd been hit. The heat of the animal warmed my palms and fingers as I stroked him. *It's okay. It's okay. It's okay.*

I laid my head on his chest, pinched my eyes shut, listened to his heartbeat slow the way I had with Mama, navigating my way around her feeding tubes. I felt the familiar, black-tar pull of death, and a deep sorrow that would age me, leave me tender to the touch. I once heard Papa say death would never get the best of him, but that was before Mama died. After she'd passed, he didn't leave the house for months, and I realized we had no control over what and who death took, only that it took us by surprise.

The glare of headlights stirred me as Papa approached with his shotgun over his shoulder. *Guess we didn't need this after all,* he said. *Help me get him on the lift.*

Together we rolled the bull's body onto burlap, then dragged him onto the lift in back of the truck.

Later that week, Papa made a stew—*nothing gets wasted*—had a taxidermist preserve the bull's head, then mounted it on the wall; and every night we ate dinner in front of the TV, watching game shows, while the elk stared at us from across the room.

For years, I dreamed about him growing inside me, a skein of horns replacing my bones, my spine, my ribs, cradling the chambers of my heart. Sometimes we'd scan the forest and mountains searching for his mother. Sometimes I'd be the dead animal pick up, lying there, seeing my mother's face staring down at me, telling me to let go, and I'd feel my fists unclench. I imagined not trembling. I imagined peace. I imagined looking into the bull's glassy eyes, hearing him say, *It's okay. It's okay. It's okay.*

To Arizona

I never felt right claiming your sun-bleached hair and sunset eyes, but that didn't stop Mama in the delivery room the night I was born. Only a 16-year-old would have the nerve to gift her fatherless child an entire state. The staff joked she was too young to understand the questions.

"What's her *name*?" the head nurse asked. "Not her place of birth, or where she was *conceived*."

"Arizona," Mama repeated, biting through a pain that had aged and stunted her.

To this day, I'm not sure if Mama had planned it that way, or if she held on to my name – our name — to spite them. Either way, you wrapped me in a coat of dust and gave me skin that held the heat. I grew a crown of thorns, anchored by a tap root Mama fastened tight to her heart, the same heart she gave too easily to men running wild in your veins. At 15, I came home to find one above Mama. His fists struck her cheekbones like thunder, when you turned my hands into lightning, cracking a skillet across his head. He slumped onto the bed Mama and I shared in the mobile home, wheezing along with the pines that combed the mountains. The paramedics kept asking him his name. One looked to me for help.

I stood with my chin held high, my knuckles knotted like juniper. A wind tore through the opened door, sweeping away the smell of iron and alcohol, erasing the small space, and I relaxed, watching with my sunset eyes, brushing back my sun-bleached hair.

"His name don't matter," I said.

We drove that night skimming the curves of your waist, feeling the pull of tides. But California was just another state with liquid coasts and horizons that didn't stay put.

"I ain't going, Mama."

She didn't argue, knowing firsthand how hard it was to leave. I drove until you pushed the sun straight into the western sky, guiding me to a copse of trees deep in the Coconino Forest. You threw a blanket over us in the evening until we woke with sweat, basking in a light you filtered through leaves, creating a new shade of green.

"It's time, Arizona," Mama said, nodding, her head staring up at the aspens and ponderosa pines, her face as fresh and young as my own.

I didn't know if she was speaking to you, me, or the face of God, but we left that day with our bones made of sunlight, heading south, carving through your army of saguaros.

Where the Hummingbirds Go

On our boulevard of weeds and rot, our retired neighbor, Ivy, made us tea and finger sandwiches, taught us chopsticks and Chopin on the piano, and doled out metaphors and buttercream mints. In the mornings, she sat outside under a canopy of wings, feeding the birds stale bread on her small patio.

"Why do so many hummingbirds come here?" we asked, her tribe of latchkey kids forming a circle around her as the birds darted toward the orange nectar she left on a low olive branch.

"Hummingbirds have a better chance of survival if they make their cone-shaped nests near the nests of hawks," Ivy said, tilting her head toward sunlight and breathing as if she were soaring through mountains. "They found their hawk."

We were used to her way of explaining the world. She made sense away from the chaos of our homes, our families, and our growing awareness that making ourselves small and unseen was both protection and a slow death. Adults on the block called her a witch, but we knew she was magical and mighty, orchestrating the wind with her knotted fingers, her untamed white hair springing loose from its many pins while she whistled birdsong. We threw crumbs with her, rolling the stale bread between our fingers as the birds flocked around us, eating from our palms, gifting us with wind and flight, sun and sky.

When the red-headed boy came over with his stepfather's fist imprinted on his cheek, we knew to get the bag of frozen peas from her icebox. We each claimed our own bag of frozen vegetables. He was asleep in the basement, and some of us were playing Candyland when we heard the knock.

"I've got it," Ivy said, flicking her wrists at us, shooing us to take cover. We flew downstairs, then tiptoed back up to watch through the cracked door, digging our nails into the wooden steps.

"Open up! I know he's in there somewhere," the stepdad yelled, pounding on the front door.

"You carry on like that, I won't answer," Ivy said. The pounding subsided, and just as she cracked the door open, the stepdad launched a kick that sent her stumbling backward.

"I ain't gotta listen to you, you crazy old hag."

Ivy pulled herself together and grew big, stretching and expanding, filling in each wrinkle of her loose skin as she took up space, pushing past the doorframe. Her house dress, a bouquet of peonies, became a garden, and the two embroidered crows, a murder.

The stepfather shrank back at the sight of her, horror streaked across his brow, his mouth agape. He stumbled backward, then turned and ran. We waited to witness what the stepfather had seen. But she shrank back into herself, closed the door, and began singing the notes she taught us on the piano, each key erasing the ink of night and the memory of our fear as we stepped on the black feathers she'd just shed, leaving a trail behind her.

If Only I Could Tell You

A wolf was in our basement last night, staring at me with his ice blue eyes as I retrieved a jug of lemonade from the refrigerator. I don't mean this metaphorically; and it's not like that time I saw the trunk of a palm tree through our hotel window and thought it was the leg of an elephant, its gray skin cracking in the tropical heat, you laughing at my wild imagination with your one martini breath on mine. It was late, yes. I took sleeping pills, I believe. Maybe I even downed a few shots of vodka and woke up parched, feeling like my body was nothing but bird feathers and spilled cartilage. Still, still, I know he was there. It was everything else that was the dream, my life wrapped around that moment. How strange it was to see a world only revealed in death, the past compressed instead of dangling, the present naked of time. If I looked away, I knew the beast would be gone, so I kept my eyes there for as long as I could, angered by the nature of momentum, taking in his sleek, snowy fur, peppered in ash. I would need to blink, to shut the refrigerator door, to walk back up the stairs, crawl into our bed, separate the sheets you always tucked in too tight, maybe wake to tell you we had a wolf in the basement. But you'd tell me I was crazy, ask me how much I had to drink, and then we'd fight, and the wolf would get lost in the story and become a metaphor, and I couldn't handle any more metaphors. So, I closed the refrigerator door, heard his nails tapping on the wood floor, following me into bed and behind my closed lids, eyeing my bird feathers, inhaling the cartilage spilling between us.

Sabrina Hicks

Home of Specimen Gardeners

3c

I'm here, I'm here, I'm here, plays on repeat, can be heard down the halls thick with the scent of pine and decay. He still walks on the soil of his youth, across the grass with cleats, dropping to his knees, burying his fingers low into the earth to fill with begonias. He loved the feel of their waxy leaves, the dangling roots, the worms wriggling below his pulse. "Wear gloves!" his mother yelled, standing at the front door on Lynnwood Drive, a matchbox starter house where they began and ended. If he'd known, he would've buried his hands deep in her abdomen, irrigated her insides, carving out the cancer. But he didn't know. None of his brothers and sisters did as they fell away like petals, leaving him alone to watch his mother's happiness smear on her lips and cheeks – the only blooms he's ever known.

2d

The day she met Rose, wishing to be the cigarette dangling from her salty mouth, was the day May stopped wishing herself away, felt the soil reach up and take hold of her ankles. Women didn't smoke like that, didn't stare long and hard, didn't hold jobs past their twenties. Rose was the exception she hadn't known existed, exhaling a steady stream of curses and wit, feeding the ground below her feet while feeding paper through a typewriter yelling, "Ed, your copy!" or, "Gary, get your lazy ass over here." Rose stole the beats from her chest, doled out the air that filled her lungs. Best friends. Sisters. Thick as thieves, *wink, wink.* Her gnarled hands linked in hers, inseparable, wedding bands from just eight years ago.

2b

She pulls his sweater down around his neck, color coordinated, mistaking volumes in his twitch, the quick tap of his index finger on the wheelchair, whisking away dust motes scattering across the dark space. His eyes are reminders of how lonesome it is in the universe, no sunlight to synthesize or roots to grasp. She spends her evenings connecting the scars on his cheeks, his forehead, his skin tag constellations, naming their shapes. She pushes them around until she has a lasting bouquet beside her, smelling past the sour layers to that place where they began. "Silvia?" he says. *Yes!* she thinks. *I'm Silvia. And you are Mine.*

Hallway

She goes home, carrying pollen with her, still wearing her scrubs, tucks in her children, her lips lingering on their cheeks. "Mom, you smell like lemons!" they say, burying their heads deep in their blankets. "You smell like the old people you take care of!" She makes a game of it, finding their ribs to tickle, their necks to kiss, their tiny bodies to cling to. All she can think is how this is slipping away, how their limbs have grown toward the sky, their feet past the quilts made years ago. *Don't grow anymore* she thinks before replacing it with *grow toward the sun*. She inhales their newness, their wonder, making her way to each of their rooms, tending to them as nights peel away the days.

Sabrina Hicks

Blink

When the rain came that morning and didn't stop until final period, I knew it would be a long bus ride home. It hadn't rained that hard since our last monsoon.

"For Christsake!" Mr. Kelly roared, as we pulled on to the ten-mile stretch of dirt road, now thoroughly soaked and slick with mud. He flashed his squinty eyes in the rearview mirror, making no effort to hide his contempt for the rural kids living forty minutes out of town. Not a mile off blacktop he began swerving and overcompensating on turns.

"You gotta stay in the ruts," Peter yelled from the back of the bus.

We'd been telling Mr. Kelly since he took over this route to stay in the ruts for traction when it rained, but he wasn't the type to listen—not to kids anyhow. He would pick us up and drop us off like he was in the sanitation business.

"We'll never make it home," I sighed, elbowing Maggie for more room, as she leaned into me with each hard turn.

"At this rate, we'll never make it to high school," Maggie said. The bus lurched forward and in one final groan, came to a halt.

"Don't move!" Mr. Kelly yelled, as the bus tilted right.

We peered out the window to find we were stuck in a ditch on the side of the road. He attempted to back up, spinning the wheels and splattering mud on the sides of the bus, but it didn't budge.

"Great," Maggie said. "Add on another half-hour for help to arrive."

The rain saturated the air with the ripe scent of manure and grass, circulating through the few windows not rusted shut, and the sun began to filter through the heavy clouds, casting a web of light around us.

Mr. Kelly heaved his weight on the patchwork seat of duct tape, foam, and torn plastic, and he tossed the CB radio aside, grumbling, "They're sending someone now. Stay put."

I sighed, watching two cows torn between curiosity and grazing, thinking they'd be the only witnesses if Mr. Kelly decided to strangle us.

"Remember our staring contests in fourth grade?" Maggie asked, as I calculated how long it would take for me to walk home. Eight miles on muddy roads didn't seem worth it.

"June? Junie?" She waved her hand in front of my face, and I swatted it away.

"Yeah. So?"

Her eyes bulged at me.

"Really? Don't you think we're a little old for that?" I said, watching them swell like spikes of golden-brown wheat in the late sun. That's how I remembered her eyes in fourth grade when I was crowned The Staring Champion, and it had been an accurate description. I remembered the eye color of most of the kids in my class at Kirkland Middle School, especially since there were only 47 eighth graders.

On our bus there was Peter Maycomb, with overcast gray eyes that, depending upon the light, cleared to a dull blue; Daisy Palmer had a mismatched set of cat eyes – green with yellow centers; and then there was Koaty Taylor, the new kid, only two days into the school year, and already I'd pegged his eyes to be as dark as a moonless night. On Monday, I watched him get on the bus for the first time, when our eyes briefly met. He then went to the back of the bus, snapped on his headphones, and slumped so low in his seat he disappeared. Rumor was he went to live with his grandmother, Betsy, a caretaker on the Buchanan's potato farm, after his mother died in a car accident and the state declared his absentee father unfit. Mama said Betsy had always disapproved of her daughter marrying a Cherokee Indian and hadn't even met Koaty until a few months ago.

Maggie's eyes drilled further into mine.

"You don't have a chance," I said, staring back at her.

Daddy liked to say my eyes were hardened from the winds coming off the plains, the kind that drove the pioneers crazy. I'd been riding fences with him on horseback, watching the sunrise every morning since I was five, training myself to push past the bitter weather and count cattle through brush.

In the first signs of fatigue, Maggie began stretching her eyelids, making them wide.

"Give up?" I asked.

"Never," she said, grimacing. She crinkled her freckled nose when I heard Daisy and Peter move to the seat behind us.

"God, I can't believe y'all are still playing that idiotic game," Daisy said.

"You got any better ideas?" Maggie replied, still staring at me.

"Truth or dare?" Peter said.

"We all know the dares *you* like, Pete," Daisy hissed.

Out of the corner of my eye, I saw him deflate, leaning back into the seat. Maggie started to twitch. Next, she'd hold her breath, and I'd win. Nothing had changed since the fourth grade, not in this town. She drummed her fingers on her jeans, blew her cheeks up, and blinked.

"What a freak you are, June! How come your eyes don't get dry?"

She began rubbing hers when Mr. Kelly waddled toward the back of the bus. We watched him as he used each seat to prop himself upright, muttering about how his entire day had gone wrong. He stopped at Koaty's seat and snapped his fingers in front of his face. "Hey, you mind taking those things off for a second?"

Koaty sat up and slid his headphones back to rest on his neck. He looked at Kelly, and, for an instant, me.

"What?"

"Move up with the rest of the kids. I'm opening the emergency door here, and I need you out of the way."

Koaty looked at the four of us staring at him and I felt the need to nod. I'd seen Mr. Kelly toss a kid off the bus last year for back talking. I could only imagine what he'd do to some new kid who sassed him.

Koaty gathered his belongings while Maggie stood up, gesturing next to me.

"First, you must beat Kirkland's Staring Champion," she said.

He looked nervous and uncomfortable as he approached, clutching his backpack and sweatshirt.

"Naw, you don't have to," I said, trying to spare him, or myself, I couldn't tell because suddenly my heart felt like a caged bird beating wildly in my chest. I thought he would sit opposite us, but Maggie was blocking the seats, and he slid in next to me, tossing his belongings at his feet. His hair blocked most of his face, but he ran his fingers through his dark, wavy curls, tucking them behind his ear, and I saw how his features were a map of two cultures. His lips were full, and his skin pale, but he had high cheekbones and a rigid bone structure, showing his Native American roots, striking an unusual and fine balance.

"Come on June," Daisy said, pounding the seat behind me. "Initiate him."

Mr. Kelly threw open the latch in back, sounding like he was going to pass out, and the bus groaned.

Peter shook our seat. "If June wins, I say we commit mutiny and get this piece of crap going again. I've driven bigger rigs than this on these roads with my dad."

I turned my body toward Koaty, noticing the small holes in his jeans and his faded, red shirt with a peeling name of a band or brand. When I reached his eyes, he was already staring at me with unnerving attention.

"It's stupid," I said. But I couldn't look away. His eyes were much darker than I thought. Not like night at all. Night always brought millions of stars. Koaty's eyes were like the abandoned, endless well I sat by as a child, wondering how deep I had to go before I'd find the world I was sure laid beyond. I remember wanting to see the water, some reflection of sky, but it was too deep and dark, swallowing stone after stone, and when I called into it, my voice dissolved into an echo.

"You're pretty good," I said, not sounding like myself. "Usually people give up right about now."

He didn't say anything. I wanted to break free of his gaze but couldn't. I tried focusing on the reflection in them, the sight of me gazing back, or the window of the bus and the field outside, but I was drawn to the darkness of his irises merging with his pupils, recalling the day I wedged my body deep inside the well, determined to find my mirrored reflection. I hadn't thought about it for years, but it always bothered me, like a meandering story with no resolution, or a book with no end.

His lashes trembled slightly, and I thought he would blink, instead his lips parted, curling to one side as he drew breath, and I wondered if he was reading my thoughts. I found dark eyes the hardest to read, but as I stared at him, I saw the cold stain of his mother dying and his father leaving, hardening him, defiant and layered in anger. His mother, however, had gifted him with softness, seen in his lips and the delicate slope of his nose. I saw the spare room he stayed in, his bed resting along the wall, near a window, in the caretaker's cabin. I had been there once before when I was little, to deliver apples to his grandmother. I imagined him staring out before sleep, bathed in moonglow and starlight. I saw his eyes pushing back, stronger than any wind, animal-like, the way a cow protects her calf. He wouldn't cry though, even when he wanted to, and suddenly I felt the contagion of his loneliness, the seed of it spreading in my gut.

Maggie and Daisy started talking about Science class, already bored of our contest, and in the background Mr. Kelly began cursing and kicking the bus. When Peter finally lost interest, Koaty said, barely above a whisper, "You have the lightest eyes I've ever seen."

I had never considered my own. They were nothing special—a basic blue. Even as he stared at me, it seemed funny he should notice. I'd always been the observer, never the observed, and suddenly I felt the heat of my body rise to my face and sting me.

"They're as big as the sky," he added.

"Yours are like the bottom of our old well," I said, before I could consider my words. I didn't want him to think I meant anything by it. But I suppose I had.

"Is there water in it?" he asked.

I nodded, sensing the importance of my response, even though I had never seen water there. I'd almost killed myself trying to find out. Looking back, I'd been reckless. The well was in a distant pasture, and I could have fallen in without anyone knowing. I remember clutching the rope, my feet climbing the stone side. But he seemed relieved by this, like I had thrown him the same line of rope.

The sun bled through the window behind me. I saw it so clearly in his eyes -- the pasture, the cows, the rolling hills beyond, and all the blue above.

"It held the sky," I said.

His lips stretched into a wide smile, and at the same time, we blinked.

Sabrina Hicks

Succession

We played hide-and-go-seek in each other's homes: dinner parties, backyard barbecues, white elephant gift exchanges. We'd steal bits of towering desserts, macarons and crème brûlée coating our teeth as we sipped the forgotten, half-drunk remains of Rosé left from our parents, counting to twenty while we scattered like leaves, making our way to the dark corners, the closets, behind the wall of shoes and thick wool coats. We inhaled musty decades of moth-eaten furs from animals that once roamed a forest, hiding in trees and bushes until plucked by a trapper, skinned and sold to adorn the delicate shoulders of the elite, until the appearance of a conscience wore better. We'd pet rabbit and mink waiting in the dark, *poor thing, poor thing,* listening to footsteps and breathing, our heartbeats drumming.

We liked being hunted, but sometimes if we hid too well, we'd be forgotten in our tight spaces, our bored hands reaching for the secrets of our parents: letters from old lovers, stacks of porn, the weight of guns. Because we folded easily, contorting our bodies until small and invisible, we'd hear their slurs, drunk off gin and vodka martinis, hear the shake and stir, the two olives straight up, the dirty and neat. Hear their affairs over the rattle of ice, their whispers down the halls as we watched them stumble hand in hand like mismatched pairs. A door closing, a lock clicking, the youngest of us holding her breath under a bed that moaned and squeaked.

We'd exchange stories in the basement to declare a winner. Celebrate with stolen bottles of Jack, matching their longing and restlessness—repulsed by them; in awe of them—vowing to be different even as we held the stems of cocktail glasses between our fingers, furs around our necks, revolvers in our hands.

We were the kids of doctors and lawyers, judges and future politicians, people used to making the rules, so we made our own. Nudie magazines out, shot glass in front. Drink, peek, and fire an empty chamber aimed up at the ceiling creaking above us, guessing our parents' footfalls.

We heard them ask: *Where are the kids?*

Playing, someone yelled and laughed. *Let them play!*

Sabrina Hicks

There Is No Advice I'd Give My 16-Year-Old Self

Because I wouldn't have skinned knees, raced cars in a swallow of city lights, tipped cows in a pasture gutted with the spill of a harvest moon. Because I wouldn't have felt a coyote's breath or the spring of snakes, danced around fires in deserts with a stumble of kids like me (nothing like me), climbed electrical towers, red Solo cup between my teeth, bitter beer running down my neck, all wanting out but not knowing where, waiting for sirens, waiting to be seen then unseen. Because rage and hope go together, and there is no self without self-loathing. Because youth is a falling, a pitch sailing toward light. It's all timing, timing, timing. Because telling myself not to worry about that boy or that boy wouldn't have led to the boy. Because the men I knew wouldn't have listened. Because all the secrets I kept are still worth keeping. Because how would I know that to love myself required walking into the ocean and drowning the takes and retakes it took to get there. Because I had no money to buy Apple. Because I never knew how to save a life. Because I would have told myself to kindly fuck off.

Walking Contradictions

Long story short, there was a kid I knew in middle school who rode the bus with me to a sprawl of desert and dirt where his family raised quarter horses, or maybe they were Arabians, and I'd watch him walk down a long dusty road in his creepers, with his saggy bottom jeans and chain bouncing off his leg, his blue hair gelled into a faux hawk like an exotic bird had landed in the desert and was trying to find its way out, and I'd think how much I wanted to get out too, that maybe we were all just birds bouncing around these self-contained greenhouses, needing a window to be opened, the way we girls imagined ourselves in a childhood game of MASH, picking a number, counting and circling our futures, whether we'd live in a mansion, apartment, shack, or house, knowing we should want the very best of the best, that shacks were ruins off an even longer dirt road, and mansions were home base, slick with city lights, but for every category we'd have to add one poor choice so we'd end up with an oxymoron, a mansion and an AMC Gremlin to put in our five-car garage, or we'd get our dream job but be forced to marry the nose picker and come home to a sniveling brood, and I'm not even sure dream job was a selection, maybe we didn't even allow ourselves to dream that big, maybe it was just number of kids we'd produce instead—cars, living arrangements, spouse, and kids—that's all for us girls in the '70s and '80s.

Anyway, I completely forgot about this boy with a blue faux hawk and pointy suede shoes, didn't think about him for entire decades as I flew away and lived along the East Coast thinking I was worldly, as if leaving your hometown makes you a better person, and maybe it does, or maybe contrast is all you crave when you're young, using it as a disguise, a gimmick, then a necessary journey to find your place, but I thought about him when I moved back and saw how much everything had changed: the desert littered with golf courses and resorts, the brittlebushes and creosote bulldozed for wine bars and luxury apartments, and that horse farm from long ago turned into a Home Depot. The whole thing didn't hit me until I needed flowers one day and found myself there in Home Depot's greenhouse looking for anything that could last in the 110-degree heat—I was standing on that dirt road where he'd walked, quarter horses or Arabians on either side of him, and I looked around at all the flowers on display, at these tropical and coastal flora wishing to be somewhere else, having no business in the desert, as if they had any chance of survival under the Sonoran sun, and I picked up a prickly pear cactus I'd been eyeing and left with it strapped in the passenger seat of my Honda Pilot, driving past the acres of grass with their sputtering sprinklers and corner sign holders, twirling ads in furry costumes under the blaze of heat hoping that boy, now a man, found a road he could walk down, his blue hair piercing the sky.

The Shedding Process

1.

Begin with the first layer. Newborn skin will not serve you. The desert child laying under citrus trees, in the hollow of paloverdes, waiting for a bird to fall from the sky. When one does, you wrap it in your palms, promising to love it until it can fly. You promise it many things while it shakes its new feathers and trembles until you're told by your brother you have just killed the baby by holding it. The mother will never come back now. Your hands, your scent, have sealed its death. He laughs while you cry. You weep for the bird. You weep for that first layer.

2.

It doesn't become easier—growing, stretching, sloughing. Beyond the ranch, you sift through an old junkyard, ruins of household items from long ago, to get away from horses and horse shit, from roping and riding, your brothers and their cowboy ways. They try to rope and drag you, hog-tie you into submission. You'd rather die, you say, all Joan of Arc. You roam as far as you can, dig through the rust of metal and tin, kick at the 1950s washing machine thinking grit isn't putting up with the bullshit of men, it's knowing when to burn down the fucking house. You kick the appliances until your toes blister in your boots. All around you is the sweat it took to build these barbed wire fences, keeping in the cattle, keeping out the coyotes, the javelinas, the mountain lions who prey upon the babies. But under the empty cans of beans, Coke bottles made with thick glass, are the bones of dead animals. Wolves always find their way in.

3.

You start to hear the rattle earned with each shedding, adding segments like notches on a belt, the tsk, tsk, tsk in the brush. Babies are silent; you've started to make noise. Down the bone-dry washes, thick with creosote and sand, you listen, watch for the coral snake, for the wrong sequence of coloring, singing: *red touch yellow, kill a fellow; red touch black, friend of jack.* You find snakes in your freezer every time you get ice. They stare back at you, reptile eyes open, coiled neat in Ziploc bags, their slick scales frozen solid. Your older brother throws his snake guards by the back door, holds up his shotgun and hollers, *Got another!* Soon, there's no room for ice. The freezer is full of dead rattlesnakes. You eat one to show you're not afraid; you're not a hypocrite; you're not soft no more. It tastes like the meat of something once alive.

4.

You shed fast and hard, planning your escape, checking maps, marking the roads leading out, stretching further every year until you're so far gone you can barely hear your roots dragging behind you like entrails. Until you do. Until you can't fit into cars. You don't fit in the trains or the city. They grow and drag and grow and drag. They grow thicker in winter and stronger in the cold. They rattle and defrost, until ice puddles and they have free range in the house, nipping at your heels until you're back where you started — under a desert sun, watching the sky for falling birds. You toss stale bread and seeds, feeling the wind on your neck as they swoop down from the eucalyptus tree, unafraid, your voice strong and silent at the ready.

Sidewinder

My first job was at a Wild West theme ranch called Tombstones, just outside of Cave Creek, Arizona. It was a dust-covered tourist trap built like the set of an old Western. My boyfriend Sam at the time worked there as a gunslinger and got me a job serving mostly sarsaparillas as a bar wench. That wasn't the official title, but it was thrown around along with barmaid, door whore, suds-slinger. This was the early 90s. No one was sensitive to titles or wording. In fact, I'm fairly certain two decades earlier I would have assumed the role of Madam and been instructed to ask every gentleman who passed through the swinging doors his type of whiskey and women.

Below the stairs in the saloon the word "brothel" was painted over with an arrow pointing up from when Tombstones first opened in 1963. Bedrooms were implied behind the painted backdrop of doors, though in an effort to be more family friendly, the hard liquor got culled and the set got whitewashed.

"Barmaid, fetch me a sarsaparilla!"

"Haha, fucker. Fetch it yourself."

"Such a sassy broad," Sam would say. "I don't know why I keep you around."

Since the day I started, it went like that. Our role-playing escalating and blurring. Tombstones had that effect.

Sam was the good guy in the white hat with five gunfights a day at high noon. High noon was at 10am, 11am, 1pm, 3pm, and 5pm. Never at noon. The town's clock tower stayed at 12, and rang twelve times before each gunfight, which were hyped to keep tourists around long enough to tour the mine, visit the petting farm, eat, and buy more western gear and memorabilia to bring back to their Midwestern and Eastern lives, claiming they saw a shootout at the OK Corral.

Christopher was the bad guy in the black hat, soft spoken, relatively new in town, a year older than me and a year out of high school. He was tall, with dirty blond hair, his face perpetually shaded by his cowboy hat, and good looking in a way that only became apparent once he lifted his head and stopped scowling. He had moved to Arizona from Montana, was good with animals, and was rumored to have turned down a full ride to a college somewhere in the South. Sam was a local boy, high school cute, the first chosen for any team. I should be so lucky I was told more than once, but I don't believe he was ever told the same about me.

Christopher started a week after I did, and worked every day, with only Mondays off, and took up smoking Marlboro Reds to look the part until he became addicted. Then they let him smoke whenever he wanted, as long as he stayed in character.

"Yo, Daisy!" Sam shouted across the dusty road by Edna's Sweet Shop. "How about a sarsaparilla? It's hot as hell out here!"

Technically I was working so telling him to go to hell was out of the question. It irritated me that he never called me by my name at the ranch. We all had stage names we were supposed to use, but hardly ever did. I wasn't Kaycee until I was off the clock. At Tombstones, I was Daisy.

"I'll get right on that," I said, rolling my eyes. Christopher had been smoking outside the saloon, leaning up against a post, which was something he often did. It made him look the part but it also suited him. He was quiet and sullen with a scowl permanently fixed between his gray eyes.

"Why you let him talk to you like that?" he asked.

I hadn't noticed Christopher there at first and he startled me. "He's just playing a role."

"He's a douche."

I considered that for a moment. I was supposed to ask Edna for more peppermints. We kept a bowl out for cafe customers and had run out. I pulled at the bodice of my dress, never comfortable in the bustier that required my breasts to spill over. I felt ridiculous and perpetually embarrassed, wondering if my $5.75 hourly wage was worth the degradation.

"He's not so bad," I offered. At that point in my life, Sam seemed pretty typical of the boys I encountered—immature and hardly worth the trouble.

Christopher continued scowling and smoking his cigarette, checking his watch to make sure he didn't miss the build-up of his high noon shootout with Sam. I began to wonder if their rivalry was manufactured or was becoming deep-seated. Christopher took to his role of loner so well I wasn't sure if it was for show either.

"He's got a rage in him," he said, focusing his eyes on me. "You should be better about spotting that." He flicked his Marlboro in the dirt, snuffed it out with his cowboy boot and headed in the direction of the goldmine where the water fountain and bathrooms were located.

I should be better about spotting that. The words bounced around in me, especially considering it was Christopher who always seemed pissed off. My father had a bit of a temper, I knew that. But so did my mother. They'd fight like hell most days and I couldn't wait to graduate. I was a senior in my last semester with only one class left so I spent most of the time working, saving up to go to college in Tucson. I hated high school, which was why I tolerated Sam. He had at least made it sort of interesting—at first. I wasn't an obvious choice for a guy like him. No cheerleading or firm reputation to speak of. Mostly, I blended in.

A large family ran past me. A mother, a father, and four kids ranging in ages from two to maybe eight. The kids had their toy guns and were shooting everything. The oldest boy aimed his gun right between my eyes. "Bang!" he yelled.

Kids did this every day at Tombstones. We were instructed to play dead or brush it off. One time Sam acted dead so perfectly a kid went screaming to his parents.

"Bang, bang, bang!" he yelled.

I wasn't about to get my dress dusty in a fall, but I planned to grab my chest and act wounded. It just took me a while. Like I had a moment of clarity at how messed up this was. I took in the prop guillotine, the scattered tombstones, the cowgirls shuffling around in their prairie skirts, boys in their pearl snapped shirts, red bandannas around their necks, cowboy hats, guns in their holsters, and got a bit lightheaded at the spectacle.

"Son," Christopher said sharply, returning from his break. "We don't go aiming at people's heads." He grabbed the end of the kid's barrel and pointed it up. "First thing about gun safety is never aim unless you intend to shoot. And we don't shoot the innocent."

Christopher was unoriginally named Black Bart. Only Sam got to keep his name for some reason. I guess the good guy's name wasn't important as long as it didn't sound bad, and Samuel was a name that worked across centuries.

The kid was holding a WANTED poster with Christopher's face on it. BLACK BART was written underneath, and there was a $500 reward for him dead or alive.

"Then you're the good guy?"

"No. I'm the bad guy," Christopher pointed at his face on the poster. "See there. I rob banks. I terrorize the town." He paused. "I kill people."

I thought back to that picture of Christopher being taken. I remembered thinking he had haunting gray-blue eyes, perfect for the role. But then he curled his lip to one side and became Black Bart.

"Then why do you care if I shoot her?"

"Because I do," he said in a way the kid didn't question. I couldn't see Christopher's face, but I saw the kid step back, wide-eyed. I scooted into Edna's shop a bit dazed. In the few weeks he'd been there, this was the most we'd spoken. He'd started as a caretaker for the animals on the edge of town before assuming the role of Black Bart, which brought him right outside of where I worked.

Inside, the room smelled of sugar and lemons. The air conditioning was on full blast which made me want to linger. It was early February and already the temperature was climbing in the desert. Sometimes we came in here to cool off, but Edna would shoo us out if we stayed too long.

"I need more peppermints," I said.

She patted at her red wig and handed me a bag of mints. "If you see Jacob, remind him I'm off early today. Four o'clock. I have a doctor's appointment."

I nodded, thanked her, and headed back outside.

Jacob Forester ran Tombstones. He was in his early 40s and was originally from Boston, a fact he tried to cover up with a terrible southern twang. Even though we were certain he'd never set foot on a real working ranch, he'd fully embraced cowboy culture and it was hard to picture him outside the fake town of Tombstones.

I scanned the afternoon crowds until my eyes settled on Christopher. He was adjusting the saddle on Wilbur, an old horse used for these staged scenes, which meant it was almost high noon and soon someone would shriek, "Sheriff! It's Black Bart!" and then all the ladies under their parasols would become hysterical, pretending to be terrified. That was Sam's cue, the best gunslinger in town, ready to challenge Black Bart to a cowboy duel. Twelve paces, turn, and shoot.

If I was outside, I was instructed to be one of the screaming ladies, which I refused to do, so I tried hurrying across the street and tripped over my skirt, landing face down in the middle of the dusty road in between the saddle shop and guns and ammo. I stayed down for a second longer making sure my breasts didn't fall out, when I felt a hand lift me up. I fell into Christopher's arms comically, as if it were part of the act. He brushed dust off my face.

"You all right, Kaycee?"

I took a few steps back, startled by the soft drawl of his voice saying my name.

"You moving in on my Daisy, Black Bart?" Sam yelled down the road, readying himself for the shootout. People began to stop along the street.

"For Christ-sake," Christopher muttered. The bell tower vibrated. "Well, showtime," he said, and I scooted out the way and back into the saloon before Jacob saw me and gave me a lecture on performing and to always remember he's paying us to remain in character.

From my station, doling out sodas and drinks, I heard the bell echo throughout town. I served my last customer a lemonade when the popping began. Sam was ad-libbing, calling Black Bart a killer, a coward, a lazy no good dirty varmint preying upon the good people of Tombstones. Jacob didn't mind his adlibs. In fact, he'd praise him afterwards, tell him he was a credit to the town. With zero sense of irony, Jacob would say, *Sam, it's men like us who'd made the West what it is today*. And when we laughed to point out the façade or the encroaching suburbs and golf courses in the desert surrounding us or how women lacked basic human rights then we'd be shut down and told: *In here, you're Daisy. In here, only the town of Tombstones exists. In here, it remains 1881.* We all knew Jacob's vision of the old West was his religion and we were to remain his disciples in his carefully constructed world.

When work was over that day, Sam and I drove to a burger place nearby. I didn't have a car so I relied on him to take me to and from work. We'd changed into our regular clothes but I still felt Tombstones stuck to my skin, carrying with it a fine dust of silt.

"What was with you and Christopher today?" Sam said before taking a bite of his burger.

"Nothing. I fell. He helped me up."

"So now he wants to be the good guy."

I took a hard look at him, noticing the twitch in his nose, the way one eye drooped slightly. Away from high school and his group of friends, it felt like I was sitting across from someone I'd just met.

"He *is* a good guy. These are just roles we're playing, Sam. White hat, black hat, they're *costumes*. You do realize that?"

"Yeah, not with him though. He really is a hick. Plus, it felt like he was putting the moves on my Daisy."

"You ever think I'm not Daisy?"

It had been like that working with him. When he was in the halls of high school, bouncing around the lunch tables, I knew who he was. Or maybe I knew who he was to me, a distinction I couldn't make right away. I was attracted to him superficially, of course. He was currency at a place where I thought I needed some.

The next weekend had started out much the same. I came out of the dressing room in costume and scanned the town for the few friends I'd made, a girl named Katy, who was a cashier at the souvenir shop, and Sarah at the ice cream parlor. Christopher was feeding the horses and cleaning out the stalls. I waved to him and he tipped his hat.

It was my job to clean out the soda machine, make the lemonade and ice tea, and get the hot dog rotisserie started, so I hurried across the street. I enjoyed getting there a few hours before the ranch opened, when the sun would sit on the mountains and linger, shaping a colorful horizon. When the sun was directly overhead, everything felt too bright and I found myself taking cover. I'd never been an early riser, and though I'd grown up in the desert, I wasn't aware of its beauty until those mornings, with the right cast of light, when everything was soft, even the cacti, their needles lit up like sun rays and the quail and doves cooing. I began to feel rooted in the land. With the ranch empty, Tombstones felt peaceful, a sleepy town where you could pretend time had stopped. Where life was as simple and uncomplicated as good and bad.

Sam had changed into his costume: hat, chaps, spurs, gun in his holster, which he'd taken to spinning and trying to get the tricks right. He'd gotten fast with his draw, though I'd noticed Christopher refraining from drawing faster. The good guy had to win.

"Stick 'em up, Daisy," Sam said, aiming his gun at my waist. I raised my hands and Sam grinned. Then he popped a cap.

"Generally, when someone surrenders you don't shoot."

"You can never be too sure." He jammed his gun in his hostler and winked at me. "Lunch later?"

The first gunfight was the least exciting. People were still gathering the lay of the land, buying tickets for pony rides, panning for gold, visiting the farm. I could hear Christopher and Sam barking out their script. It seemed strange to hear Christopher speak so much. Generally, he never spoke outside his lines, and during his lunch break he'd eat in the barn with the horses. He took great care of them, brushing their coats and checking their hooves when he didn't have his shootouts. I'd heard he lived with his father, who was a farrier, and had taught Christopher the trade of shoeing horses.

I began finding excuses to run into him. Jacob had called a meeting after work that day and I volunteered to tell Christopher in the barn.

"What does he want this time?" Christopher asked.

"He said something about stepping up our game. Getting more people through the door."

Christopher was brushing a horse named Roscoe. He shook his head. "That guy."

"You don't like anyone," I said, joking.

He stopped brushing. "I like horses."

"You must have grown up around them in Montana."

"I grew up on ranches, so yeah." Roscoe nudged him and he started brushing again.

"Is your mom still there? In Montana?"

His face tensed up. "No, she took off when I was young."

"Sorry," I said, quietly. I watched him run his hands down the horse's sides and underbelly.

He tipped his hat back. "Anything else?"

That's how it was for a while. Me seeking him out, learning bits and pieces of his life. He lived with his father, had no siblings, didn't seem to remember his mother. They moved around a bit. He loved reading and had done well in school. He was nineteen, and talked about college, but in a vague way. He seemed to have no friends or family outside of his father, and even that relationship I gathered was strained. But mostly, he turned every question around and I ended up doing the talking, telling him about my parents, my sister in college. And just when it seemed we were forming a friendship, or I got him to smile or laugh, he'd shut down and try to avoid me. I began to think I was bugging him until I stood cooling off in Edna's Sweet Shop one Friday. I lingered by the air conditioning pretending to be reading an old newspaper we had made up with fake headlines about cattle rustlers.

"Don't think for a minute I don't know what you're doing," Edna said, hauling out candy from the backroom.

"Well then let me help you while I cool down," I said, fanning myself. "I absolutely hate these ridiculous dresses. They're restricting, they keep in all the heat, and I look like a prostitute! How did women do it back then?"

Edna laughed. "Back then it was a burden just being a woman, even for a pretty girl like yourself. Maybe even more so. Still is a burden, if you ask me." She tossed me a bag of taffy to refill the bins and looked out the store window. "Which one of them boys are you dating?"

"Sam," I said.

"Is he the one who's always looking at you?"

I shook out the last of the candy and joined her. I pointed to Sam. "The guy who plays the good guy." Sam was strutting around with a toothpick in his mouth, grabbing his gun from his holster to twirl.

"That's not the guy who's always looking at you," she said. Then she pointed to Christopher. "That's who I'm talking about."

Christopher was avoiding Sam, smoking his Marlboro, running a lariat rope along the railing and hitching posts.

"He does that. Looks for you, then settles down a bit, knowing where you are."

"You're kidding me," I said, pulling back the curtain.

"Nope. I'm not. He'll do that until he finds you. I see everything from this shop, believe me." Edna raised her eyebrows, then winked at me. "So your boyfriend is the good guy in the white hat?" Edna seemed to relish this news. "I like the bad guy better. But then again, I never trust anyone claiming to be a good guy. If I learned anything in these 73 years, it's that anyone claiming to be good and holy ends up being the worst."

After work that day we gathered around the guillotine for another meeting. Jacob, we all knew, had a gun fetish. He had friends in Hollywood who'd set him up with a new collection of prop guns. "No more caps," he said. "These guns take blanks you'd swear are the real deal." He was thinking of adding blood packs underneath the shirts for the shootouts just like they did on the movie sets. "Sam, great job today," he added. "Christopher, remember, you're on a rampage. You're trapped. You ain't getting out alive, but you ain't going out quietly either. I need more." Sam was sitting next to me, playing with a prop gun Jacob had brought out, spinning the barrel and before I knew what was happening, Christopher grabbed it out of his hand and set it hard on the guillotine stage.

"What the fuck is the matter with you?" Sam said standing up.

"If you had any goddamn sense, you'd know you never point a weapon at anyone."

"I wasn't pointing it at anyone."

"You were pointing it at Kaycee." Christopher looked at me and I could feel the blood rushing in my ears.

"It's a prop gun, asshole, not a weapon, and the chamber's empty."

Christopher's jaw tightened and no one spoke.

"I think this has more to do with her," Sam said, stepping back, widening his chest. "What? You want a shot at my girlfriend?"

I stood between them and pushed Sam. "Go to hell," I hissed.

"All right, all right," Jacob finally said. "Use all that bad blood for tomorrow and make it good!"

Everyone started gathering their stuff, eager to get out of there. Jacob had kept us late and he wasn't going to be paying us overtime.

"You can find your own ride home," Sam said to me. "Maybe he can take you." And then, as he walked away debating the level of hate he wanted to unleash, "Just so you know, she doesn't put out."

That night, I wasn't going to accept a ride from Christopher, though he offered. I was humiliated. Sam knew exactly where to strike; what girls carry around with us from when we are little. How much of ourselves can we give away as we step into adulthood. It was a constant calibration. One boys never had to make. I did not love Sam. I knew that even then. But I realized then I hadn't even liked him. He was just the artifice I had grown accustomed to.

I waited on the curb for my mother to pick me up. And Christopher, I knew, didn't leave the ranch until she came, when everyone left one by one. He tried to be discreet but I saw his blue Ford truck pull out behind us, turning in the direction of his home.

I hid most of the next day, staying behind the bar, watching a few tourists file in and leave. When Christopher passed the saloon window, I caught him looking in and motioned him inside.

"I'm sorry about yesterday," I said.

"What do you have to be sorry for? Sam's the jackass." He looked around the empty saloon and sat down at a bar stool. "So, you're broken up?"

I picked up the bar towel and threw it down. "Definitely. It was overdue."

He smiled and spun around slowly. "You let me drive you home tonight?"

I hesitated.

"Not that you need a ride or anything," he trailed off.

I nodded. "Sure, that'd be great."

He tipped his hat. "Come find me in the barn when you're ready."

I began watching the gunfights after that, standing outside the saloon with the others, noticing the way Christopher's face changed when he drew his gun, hesitant with a forced delay. He was much faster than Sam, but he never pulled the trigger, not once, though he had time. Jacob would tell him, "We need more gunfire. More noise! More blood and guts." But Christopher still never fired off his gun, so Sam overcompensated, blasting away.

When I reached the barn at the end of the day, I found Christopher in his street clothes looking like a modern-day cowboy in jeans, button down, and boots. He looked sad in the light, crouched in a squat, leaning against a post, smoking. Next to him was his black cowboy hat.

"Why the bad guy?" I asked.

"What do you mean?"

"Why did you choose that role?"

"The role chose me."

"I don't believe that for a second."

"Well you don't know me."

"Yeah, you won't let that happen."

Christopher had started out as caretaker of the animals, then signed up to fill the role of Black Bart when the guy who'd played him left. But Christopher wasn't an actor type. We had a handful of those. People who put on a show with flair and effort. Sam was a natural showboat. Christopher, playing any role was at odds with who he was, but he made people stop and stare. His face transformed when he shouted his lines, taking on a vulnerability of self-loathing and hatred that was hard to look away from.

"There's freedom in not trying to win people over. You just," he threw his hands out, "lean into the role, or a past you cannot escape."

"And what past is that?"

Christopher didn't respond. He wrapped his arms around his knees and looked down.

"A past you can't recover from?"

"Kaycee," he said, hesitating. He took a drag of his cigarette and blew the smoke out of the side of his mouth. "What happens if you've done something so terrible, you have no chance at happiness."

"You couldn't have done anything that bad, Christopher. I'm sure of it."

"Are you? How would you know? No one really ever knows anyone." Christopher drew a circle in the dirt next to him. "Even my father is full of lies."

I knew I had to tread lightly or he'd spook.

"I know this. You told me I need to be better at spotting rage. The thing is, I can. Sometimes violence chooses us and we adapt. But whatever happened in your past isn't who you are now. Maybe it never was."

The last of the day's light filtered through the barn, a burnt orange glow of dust stretched across the hay bales, slowly settling around us.

"What about forgiveness?" I offered.

His eyes softened and watered. He scoffed and dropped his cigarette, grinding the stub into the dirt. I crouched down in front of him and he stood up defensively, taken aback. It was an odd reaction until I saw how scared he was. I took my time drawing him into a hug. He smelled of cigarettes and soap, horse hide and dust from the day. He had on a thin flannel shirt despite the heat. My head rested on his shoulder and his body released. He slowly held me back.

We stayed like that for a while, with the sun softening and the heat from our bodies turning to sweat. The horse noises and horse flies buzzing in the haze of evening. After a while I could tell he was holding back tears, gripping me tighter. The horses neighed and ground their teeth in the hopes we'd dig into the piles of grain and feed them handfuls.

I buried my face into Christopher's shoulder feeling his body twitch, and I wondered if he'd ever been held. I had assumed he'd had girlfriends. I had assumed over the course of his life people were drawn to him the way I was, but I knew then I was wrong. He wouldn't have allowed that. I felt his loneliness and pulled back to kiss his cheek, like I was consoling a child, until I felt his breath deepen and his hands tighten around my hips. All the times I had been with Sam, I had calculated all the stops, the limits before I'd push him away. That went away with Christopher. He felt like rain in the desert, when water beads up on the creosote and suddenly the desert transforms into something colorful and fragrant.

"Don't you dare give me a reason to stay," he said, breathing into my neck, combing back my long hair.

I could say for certain there was no rage in Christopher, only a rage he felt toward himself. At that moment I was afraid of losing him and the way he made me feel, and I held on tight. And maybe that love was tied to his brokenness, how it had softened and humbled him, made him feel like the safest place to land.

"What did you mean by that?" I said, as we lay with our bodies pressed together on the hay bales; the horse blanket underneath us scratching our bare skin. "A reason to stay?"

"Nobody stays in one place for long, Kaycee," he said, kissing behind my ear.

"Well, you're staying," I said, pulling him on top of me, kicking up hay.

He chuckled and pinned me down. "You look like a sidewinder, covered in dust," he said, gently brushing flecks from my face.

I ran my fingers through his sandy hair, feeling the grit of day. "A sidewinder in camouflage. That's how they get their prey."

The next day everyone had to come in early to make sure inventory was set and the grounds were watered to reduce the amount of dust; dust being a constant source of frustration for Jacob. Christopher had dropped me home late, then turned around to pick me up and we were both tired, but we dragged ourselves in, changed and went to find the other staff. Most Sundays the younger staff would sit and watch the sun come up in the desert by the shooting range, lounging on the bales of hay and lawn chairs, drinking coffee or hot cocoa from the shop in town. We'd watch the coyotes or packs of javelinas make their way through the dry washes. Sam was in one of the lawn chairs, aiming his gun at the animals trotting by, popping off caps to scare them, talking about all the times he'd killed snakes. He was irritating everyone. It had been two days since we'd broken up and he could sense I was already with Christopher.

"Would you quit?" Katy said. "I'm trying to enjoy the peace."

"Calm down," Sam groaned. "It's just a bit of target practice."

"And if there were real bullets in there?"

"Too bad I ain't got any."

"Or what? You'd slaughter the animals just going about their day?"

Christopher took out one of the lawn chairs and sat next to me. "I bet you wouldn't do shit with a real bullet."

Everyone got silent and I looked to change the subject. But Sam leaned over to stare at Christopher. "Naw, if I had a real bullet, I'd save it just for you, Christopher."

A smile spread across Christopher's face. "I'm gonna hold you to that."

I was with Christopher every evening after that, offering to close up the town. I told my parents I had to work late for inventory. Because Christopher took care of the livestock, Jacob had trusted Christopher to lock up and leave whenever we wanted. When I was with him, he wasn't filled with self-loathing, scowling in his role, hardening himself in the way he did on the dusty streets of Tombstones. With me, he was most himself. And he was beautiful.

One night we lost track of time and accidently fell asleep and I woke to him moaning and thrashing. When I shook him awake, his face was twisted in pain. I hadn't experienced anything in my life at that point that would allow me to understand. He could barely breathe. It took a lot to calm him, to reassure him he'd been dreaming, and when I asked him what it was about, he said he didn't remember. I didn't know if it was true or not. I just held him until I felt something so dark inside him it scared me to know.

After that night, Christopher's behavior became more erratic. His gunfights changed too. His draw had grown more reluctant and when he fell and looked up at the sky, he no longer looked at peace. He looked scared. I watched Christopher die five times a day and each time it struck me, there was a darkness in him shaking loose.

The first Saturday of May, the town of Tombstones was covered in a thick new layer of dust. A strong wind had swept through early that morning and filled the streets with a gritty, orange haze. Jacob postponed the first two gunfights, said when the dust settled we'd start at noon—real noon. The place was packed with people and I was busy behind the bar. I served up my last sarsaparillas and root beer float before sneaking outside. The script remained the same. Sam taunting Black Bart. Black Bart rattling through a list of his high crimes and robberies.

Christopher got through his lines okay, but when he turned to walk the twelve paces, his eyes locked on to mine, filling me with a dread I couldn't understand. I started shaking my head, telling him no as if my body knew before my brain. A few people turned to look at me and smile, thinking it was part of the act. By the time he got to twelve my heart was racing. He hesitated for a moment, his eyes still set on me, sad and scared.

"Christopher!" I yelled, his name hitching in my voice. "No!"

He dropped his gun, held up his hands and yelled, "Wait! I surrender!"

Just as he turned, Sam fired five rounds.

I knew when Christopher fell. The way he fell. It was too real, too broken. A hush ran through the crowd, then a strange scattering of applause came from both sides of the street as Christopher began bleeding out. I ran to him, threw myself over his body, screaming and shaking him. His gray eyes open, staring at the sky. No one knew if it was part of the act.

"Call 911!" I yelled, sobbing. "Someone help him!"

Sam dropped his gun and walked over to us. He looked down at him in horror.

"Jesus Christ! That has to be a blood pack, right? Jacob must've set this up." Sam fell to his knees. "This isn't real! This isn't fucking real!"

It took an investigation to piece together what I'd known, that Christopher slipped real bullets into Sam's gun. But it wasn't until I met his father, Ed, that I finally understood.

Ed handed me Christopher's journal when I went to visit him. I leafed through the pages, seeing his handwriting for the first time. I saw my name throughout the book.

"You're the only girl he's ever talked about." Ed sat on the edge of Christopher's bed. "What happened was my fault. All of it." It took Ed some time to collect himself. I sat in a chair across from him, trying my best not to fall apart.

"Christopher had a younger brother, Ryan," Ed continued. "When Chris was four years old he got a hold of my gun. I didn't have it locked up. His brother had gotten a cap gun for his third birthday and they were playing around. The gun went off." Ed wiped his eyes.

"The worse thing about it, when his mother left a few months later, I saw how confused he was, how he wouldn't stop asking when everyone was coming home. Every moment of the day: *Where's Rye? Where's Mama?* I couldn't handle it. That's on me, too. I told him he'd never had a brother. That it had been a dream and that his mother left cause she didn't want to be married to me no more. It felt like the only way he'd recover was not knowing."

I stared at the blanket on Christopher's bed, a pattern of cowboys on horseback, guns drawn toward a setting sun..

"I'd spent my life protecting Chris from a secret I knew he couldn't live with. But a few months before we left Montana, someone had known. When word got out, he went to the library and found a newspaper article," Ed sighed, and wiped his hands on his knees. "Deep down, he'd always known. He had nightmares, you know. Bad ones."

I nodded, remembering the night he was inconsolable. In the back of Christopher's journal there was a folded article. Ed shook his head when he saw it. "It was gruesome. His mother fell apart. I did the only thing I could when she took off. Left Tennessee and everything behind. Found some work on a farm in North Dakota, then Montana, places where no one knew."

After Christopher's death, Tombstones closed. The land was sold to a developer and it became another subdivision with a golf course. Sometimes I drive by the area and it hits me all over again. I picture Christopher's gray eyes casted down on me in the barn, his lip curled to one side, while the town of Tombstones slept, bidding its time under a thick blanket of dust.

Other times, in the early mornings, I head outside, root myself in the desert, waiting for the sun to hit the mountains just right, to bleed through the needles of the chollas and watch them light up like golden rays. I inhale the fragrant sagebrush and creosote, watch the outline of the saguaros turn into a posse of cowboys with their hands up, and I convince myself they're all Christopher—surrendering.

Clementine and Dally

It took a while to convince Dally to come with me to a honky tonk in Fort Worth, Texas to see Daryl Benson and the Boone Dogs sing about whiskey and women. Last time I roped her into a road trip she did a year in a Wyoming penitentiary. But Daryl was getting famous for a hit called "Old Clementine" and me being the Clementine he was singing about, I thought it only proper to pay him a visit. Hard to resist a voice with all that honey. Course he didn't need to be putting *old* before my name when I was just twenty-three. *Old Clementine, chestnut hair, eyes like sea glass, legs like a mustang,* or some horseshit like that. Clementine would have been just fine.

Funny how people can walk away from the same situation with two different stories. He sang about pining for me when he was the one who left, and I swore if I ever saw that dirtbag again, I'd sink a bullet into his growing gut. But I don't care how you cut it, hearing my name with the whine of a pedal steel guitar had me breaking all sorts of rules I'd set out to keep, not to mention parole.

Dally was living in Jerome, an old Arizona mining town that used the ashes of its miners to build the foundation. Said she liked driving on roads paved with bones and skipping on sidewalks sealed with the dead. She was wildly superstitious. Said she was as haunted as the town, making all sorts of jewelry with evil eyes to ward off the bad spirits. It was popular with the tourists there and she was able to rent a little yellow house perched on top of the town that overlooked the whole valley. Said she could see the red rocks of Sedona from her porch.

As I drove there to fetch her, I worried she'd think I was up to no good, though I'd assured her on the phone I'd tried to put those days behind me. I never started anything with bad intentions, bad intentions just seemed to find me, even when I wasn't lookin'. I'd served some time for a misunderstanding five years ago, one that involved arson and a stolen vehicle, and perhaps a dead body, but that's another story. And are you really stealing from a dead man? I reckoned he no longer had use for any worldly possessions. Of course, courts didn't see it that way. It took even more convincing that I didn't shoot him neither. Only thing I had no business doing was roping Dally into the mess. By the time they sorted it all out she'd already been behind bars for close to a year on account of having a shitty lawyer in a shitty town, with a judge old as dirt.

Anyway, I wrote her everyday asking for forgiveness. Lucky for me, she's a softer soul. We're more like sisters on account of us both being orphans and growing up together in the same rotten town. She wrote back, "Clemie, the judge told me judgment comes from experience and experience comes from bad judgment." Dally really took that to heart, bless her soul, cause if I'm being honest, I only learned to run faster than the law.

"Where to this time, Clementine?" she said, sitting on her porch waiting for me, watching the sun rise, drinking coffee and smoking a Marlboro. She handed me a cup and lit me up a cigarette. I sat next to her, making sure she knew the truck I drove there hadn't been stolen, that I borrowed it from my friend Yotes and we wouldn't be on a highway that led to the Grand Canyon, contemplating our poor life decisions with a trail of cops after us like Thelma and Louise.

"Got money?" she asked.

"Five hundred, plus a credit card."

"You steal it?"

"Yes, ma'am," I said. "Lifted a wallet last night from a loud mouth drunk at the bar I tend." She laughed. But I wasn't kidding. No sense in arguing he had it coming. Most likely the card was canceled by now, though I planned to test it at a gas station. I was in between bartending jobs anyway, which, with my prickly disposition, wasn't exactly lucrative. Having a record didn't give me many options. I was thinking I could shake Daryl for some song profit. Crooning my name without some royalties or some form of compensation didn't seem right. Figured I could seduce and negotiate with the man better in person.

"Where we heading, then?"

She handed me a lit cigarette.

"A honky tonk in Fort Worth called Billy Bob's," I said, taking a drag, thinking there was no sense in telling her I'd quit smoking. "Straight shot across New Mexico, then four hundred miles to Fort Worth, which is about six hours. They got good wings, I'm told."

"They got sawdust on the floor?"

"I don't know, Dally!" I said, blowing smoke off to the side. "What's that matter?"

"I swore off those places, that's why."

"Honky tonks, or honky tonks with sawdust?"

"Establishments with sawdust. It's bad luck for me. Plus, I'm allergic."

Sometimes tryin' to reason with Dally was like reasoning with the same girl I met in middle school. I pulled out my cell and called the bar to confirm their flooring. Guy who answered sounded like he'd just woken up. Then he mumbled something about line dancing and boots digging into wood floors and how Friday nights sounded like a stampede of cattle. Said sawdust mixing with spilled beer would be like shoveling horseshit out of a pen every night. "No!" he yelled and hung up.

"Okay. They don't have sawdust."

"One more thing," she said. "There's a diner I'd like to go to in Dallas. That's not far from Fort Worth. Heard they have the best pancakes in the whole world and the biggest too." Then she took off one of her bracelets and motioned for my wrist. I rolled up my sleeve and she secured the clasp.

"Mighty kind of you," I said, staring at the beads and evil eye in the center. "Aren't these a Greek thing?"

"Yeah, but there's no telling with my lineage. I might be a hundred percent Greek!"

"I doubt it, blondie."

I looked out at her beautiful view, took the last drag and snuffed out my cigarette before I'd start wanting another. The sun was almost fully up on the horizon floating in a pool of orange and pink. "So, you're up for the ride if we scoot over to Dallas for some pancakes?"

"Course, I am," she said, tapping my mug with hers. "We're Dally and Clementine, Clementine and Dally! Besides, I already told my landlord to keep an eye on the place. But you better leave that bracelet on for good luck. I don't have to remind you about the last time we crossed state lines."

Before I could launch into another apology she stopped me.

"Best thing that ever happened to me, Clemie. I wouldn't be here." She motioned to the view before us, high on a mountaintop with an endless stretch of Arizona sky. "You see, I got a view of my very own canyon. And ain't it grand!"

"Proud of you, Dally," I said, tapping her mug before we finished.

Fort Worth was a thousand miles east on old Route 66. We didn't stop to sleep until we hit Quay County, New Mexico just before the Texas border. The credit card was paying for the gas so I took a gamble and used it for a motel, courtesy of Bradley P. Evans who, bless his heart, hadn't gotten around to reporting it stolen. Dally and I watched cops shows in the motel and ate pizza until we fell asleep. Yotes' truck, which Dally and I renamed Lil' Blue, was holding up just fine in spite of her age, but she was making some noises when we crossed into Texas like she was trying to warn us about the Lone Star state. We were close to a little town outside of Amarillo when she finally gave up.

I called Yotes and told him Little Blue broke down.

"You mean Bonnie! She broke down because you renamed her and you had no right, Clementine!"

Now Yotes was sounding like Dally with all that superstitious nonsense and he was blaming me for his lack of maintenance. I was still yapping on the phone with him while Dally looked under the hood like she knew a thing or two about how vehicles worked. Course when I was with Dally there would be no shortage of knights in shiny armor whooping and hollering, asking if she needed help, which was good cause we needed help. Bad because the help that usually came was the wrong kind.

"Howdy pretty ladies."

Turns out one slick bastard finally stopped and I didn't like the make of his hat, which is what my mama said when she didn't trust someone. When he said ladies, he was only looking at Dally, because if he looked at me, I was cutting my eyes into him like they were a pair of steaks, thinking it was a real possibility I'd be heading back to prison. That I'd have no problem pulling my piece on a person deserving.

"Can I help you?" he said with a drawl that made me aware I was in Texas, which was agitating me to begin with. Nobody I ever liked came from Texas, but it occurred to me then Dally was short for Dallas, even though she ain't ever been, and nobody who ever knew her called her that.

"Unless you're a mechanic, I'd say best you keep to the road, cowboy."

Dally scowled at me for the remark. I was still behind the wheel of the truck but I saw her eyes from the crack under the lifted hood. Now I know it ain't fair or rational, but I got mad at Dally for being the type of woman who attracts too much attention. I swear she was a real liability. I'd been blessed with lesser looks and people left me the hell alone the way nature and God intended.

Yotes was still talking and I heard him say overheated carbonator and that we'd run her into the ground, poor old Bonnie Blue, yak yak yak. I wrapped my hand around my little .22 that I kept in the door pocket, debating on whether I needed to shoo this man away with lead.

Dally was talking with the guy, exchanging information, then shouting, we need to let the carbonator cool down, the coolant was low.

"We need to put some water in it once it settles down," she yelled. "That should get us to the next gas station. They'll have some coolant."

I was feeling pretty impressed with Dally. Seemed like she was schooling this yokel who took to following her around like we was back in a schoolyard. I didn't know how she put up with it. I would've lost my patience and told him he'd be regretting his life's choices if he didn't see himself back to his truck. Dally said I was impatient though, and I believed her to be correct.

"Okay, the smoke seems to have quit," I said. "Pour some water in and I'll start her up!"

Old Yeller, which is what I took to calling this imbecile who pulled over and offered nothing but confirmation on problems Dally already solved, began barking at me to turn the engine and I was close to pulling my piece on him just out of annoyance. But when the engine started up, I was overjoyed.

"Get in, Dally!" I yelled.

She slammed down the hood and I saw a big grin on her face.

"See, Clemie! I know my way around an engine!"

"You sure do," I said. When she got in the cab that jackass started hovering in her window with his head inside.

"You have to go so quickly?" he asked. But when he looked at me, he understood we weren't seeing eye to eye. "How about I follow you ladies to the next gas station to make sure you make it there okay?"

"The only way you make it out of here okay is if you get your head out of my truck."

Old Yeller scowled at me, then inches away from Dally's lips he asked, "How about a kiss, then?"

I pulled my .22 on him and Dally shrieked. Old Yeller backed away with his hands up.

"How about you kiss my ass," I said.

"Whoa, Betsy," he said. A sick smile curled up his lip and I put Old Blue in drive and floored it. Ran right over the man's toes.

In the rearview mirror he was hopping around on one foot like a fool, cursing us.

"Dally!" I yelled. "You attract the worst bunch of losers I'd ever seen!"

"Don't I know it!" she said laughing, the wind whipping around our hair.

Now in spite of its unoriginal name, Billy Bob's in Fort Worth was known to pull in some of the biggest names in country music and claimed to be the biggest honky tonk in the world, but I was finding out there was no place in that state claiming anything but their great size in nature. Judging how packed it was, I was impressed Daryl landed a gig there. Dally and I checked into a motel and paid cash. If Bradley P. Evans ever reported his card, I didn't want to find out in person, seeing how I was breaking my parole. I planned to be back in the Grand Canyon State before anyone knew I was gone. Dally and I got gussied up for our night out. She did my makeup because I was no good at such things, but I wanted Daryl to see me in the crowd and know I meant business. Reckoned when I saw him I'd know what to do, whether to punch him or take him to bed. Clementine, young or old, wasn't for sale, at least not without some negotiations.

There's a feeling that crawls up my spine when I enter these types of establishments, something that makes me both uneasy and excited. Maybe it's a feeling like the night can only go two ways and there ain't much in between. You either come out on top or end up digging yourself an early grave. If I was being honest, I had a bit of a weakness for cowboys, even with all their bravado and horse-kicked brains. You just had to be mighty selective with that lot, weed out them good old boys, which was no easy feat. Billy Bob's was overflowin' with a stampede of folks, all waiting to see a man I had history with when he was just an unknown, strumming his guitar, playing songs no one ever heard of at Johnnie Ray's, the hole in the wall where I'd been bartending. I'd been plying him with free whiskey when he came home with me and proceeded to sleep for two straight days. Turned out he'd been on the road so long, he'd forgotten what a bed felt like. When he finally woke, we fooled around and he started singing songs about me. I guess I should feel proud he spent more time in Phoenix than any other city til then. Musicians ain't long term lovers, but sometimes I just can't help myself and I take to pining the wrong lot.

The honky tonk was loud and packed and I'd started worrying maybe I wasn't the Clementine he was crooning about because sure as day my eyes weren't the color of sea glass, which was a lyric he used to describe me. I was a brown-eyed girl, same as all the brown-eyed girls dancing around to that one song about us down in the hollow. Plus, there were plenty of women lining up to see him, all in their tight blue denim and ruby red lips. Got me so nervous I started ordering whiskeys for Dally and me like we was hell bound when I should have been on my best behavior, remembering if I got in trouble with the law, they'd send me back to the woman's correctional center and I knew quite a few women there who'd be more than happy to make me eat dirt. Now being a bartender, you'd think I knew it was always better to be the one serving the drinks than doing the drinking. It seems my memory is short and every once and awhile I need a good reminder that I am the worst kind of drunk out there—loud, attention seeking, and ornery as a rattlesnake in a corner.

Next thing I knew I was challenging two men to a drinking contest, which caught the attention of a man in a medical boot, who pointed the end of his crutch at me and yelled, "That's the bitch who ran over my foot!" And that got me laughing so hard I fell over in my chair, and while Dally was picking me up off the floor trying to protect me, my song came on—*old Clementine hell raiser of mine.* Hearing my name sung had me busting my way toward the stage with a knot of men carrying pitchforks, gunning for me as I yelled, "Keep away, Old Yeller, you dumb sonofabitch!" I thought if I could just reach Daryl, he'd put a stop to it, but there were bouncers that got a hold of me. I thrashed my way free as a full bar room brawl broke out—bar stools flying, bottles breaking, all that nonsense.

I couldn't seem to find Dally in that tangle of human bodies slipping and sliding in beer and sweat. I ended up on stage, which is strange considering all the bouncers swearing at me, drooling like a bunch of rednecks. I heard my name being called over and over. It was Daryl telling folks I was indeed his hell raising Clementine and before I got all weepy about it, cause he remembered me, he pulled me backstage to avoid the bouncers and cops. I told him I needed him to fetch Dally, that I wasn't going nowhere without her and then she showed up looking about as rough as I felt. Blond hair a rat's nest, a shiner forming on her eye, a bloody lip, and I just knew I looked worse for wear.

And then it was morning!

I mean, I can't remember anything beyond that, which I know sounds like a cop out. But honest to God, I come from a long line of black-out drunks. Even happen to be the product of one. Mama didn't know who my daddy was, and none of the possibilities were worth pursuing. Sometimes not giving a damn is better than knowing the truth.

Dally and I slept on a couch backstage and woke up surrounded by band equipment and more bottles of beer than I could count, filling the air with a sour punch to the gut that sent me to the bathroom to make peace with the porcelain. There was a note Daryl left, telling me he had to be back on the road for another gig in Nashville that was really important and he was sorry he didn't get much of a chance to catch up. He wrote down his number and told me to call him. My head was pounding and I was filled with a loathing only a hangover can produce, but I was more upset at having missed my opportunity with Daryl.

With the little bit of hindsight I have now, I can confess I was a bit more interested in the settlement of my heart than any financial compensation. A bartender once told me to stay away from politicians and musicians, and especially writers, because there ain't nothing they all love more than words.

Dally stood up, wobbling a bit, looking like she got run over by the stampede of drunkards, trying her best to reassure me that if it was meant to be, it would have worked out and that the universe had other intentions.

"You've been stuck in that hippie town too long, Dally! The universe has no plan! Next thing I know, you'll be clamoring on about vortexes or some shit like that. I done messed up and missed my chance! Goddamn whiskey and shitty beer." I stumbled back from the bathroom and sat on the edge of the sunken couch with my head hung low.

Dally sat next to me and rubbed my back. "No, you didn't, Clemie. Your evil eye bracelet kept the cops away, we got ourselves a story, and you got yourself another song." She held up Daryl's note and on the back were lyrics about me tearing up the place. "And you know what?" she said. "I think that's what you really came here for. To hear your song. But you got one even better. You got yourself two songs!"

"Great," I moaned, but deep down I knew no good would've come from starting up something with a man on the road. Willie, Waylon, and Cash sang warning songs about that. And sometimes you can ruin a song with the truth. Maybe I was better left as a memory in that man's head, cemented into a greatness I could never live up to. "I can't wait to hear it," I said, sounding a bit more optimistic. Billy Bob's was happy to see us go and there was a man grumbling about how lucky we were to not be in jail and if we didn't know Daryl, that's exactly where we'd be. I tipped the hat I stole from someone last night and told him to stick it where the sun don't shine.

"Let's go clean up at the motel and get us some big ol' Texas pancakes," I said to Dally. "I need to get out of this rotten state before someone throws me into the Rio Grande."

Dallas was less than an hour away. Dally and I washed up, covered our shiners, and tried to tame our hair after the Billy Bob brawl. We cackled the whole way there about Old Yeller coming after us, hobbling away on his boot fixing to kill me, and I swear that song about me came on the radio, which only fueled us more. Aside from our brains swimming in a sea of stale whiskey, we were having the time of our lives, until we got close to this diner Dally was crowing about, then she started acting squirrelly, looking in the mirror to make sure her concealer was sticking and her lipstick was perfect. I even joked, "Is there someone there you want to impress?" And she got real defensive.

The diner looked like most diners I know. Booths saddled up to big windows and an all-female serving staff with pinned up hair, tight gingham tops, and flared skirts. A backdrop of male cooks was sweating in a steam of bacon grease, slinging plates through a slot. Only thing different were the signs bragging about how big their pancakes were. I was smack talking Texas about size insecurity when I noticed Dally was so nervous she was buzzin' like an electric wire. I followed her into the restaurant, heard her ask for someone's table.

"Who'd you ask for?"

"No one," she said, sitting down. I sat across from her trying to read her mind, but she looked a million miles away, which had me calibrating if I should pump the gas or apply the brakes. It's the same look she had when I first met her in Ms. Buckley's English class in seventh grade not long after I lost my mama to a car accident. I recognized the look back then. Same look of grief and abandonment, and I knew then we'd be best friends. There's nothing stronger than two people grieving together, easing the burden of having to pretend. You just never realize how much of a show you put on for people until you meet your people.

I kept quiet, pretending to be interested in the pictures of petrified toast and stacks of glistening pancakes, but when our server came to ask if we wanted coffee, I knew I was looking at Dally in fifteen or so years. The woman was tall and skinny, same cornfield blond hair and sky-blue eyes. Same heart shaped face and dimpled cheeks. Seemed she had a suspicion too 'cause she didn't take her eyes off Dally. I read her nametag: Kendra. We ordered our coffees and off she went.

"Dally, when was the last time you saw your mama?"

"Two," she said, plainly. "You know that."

"I might have known that, but then again, you told me you wanted the world's biggest pancakes and I'm suspecting that ain't the case."

"What are you saying, Clemie?"

"Is that woman your mama?"

Dally's eyes got misty and I reached for her hands. "Why didn't you tell me?"

"Cause I didn't know for sure," she said. "I did some diggin' online and found she might be here in Dallas working at this diner."

A busboy came and set down some waters.

"You think that's her?" she asked. "Her name is Kendra Hayes, but that might be common. Maybe there's another Kendra here too. On another shift. Or maybe I got the wrong diner."

Funny how the mind can trick our eyes, make us question even something that obvious, but even I didn't want to say for sure.

"Only one way to tell," I said. "You gotta ask her."

Kendra came by with our coffees and we watched her set them down with shaky hands. She steadied herself on the table and took in Dally's face. They stared at each other until she whispered, "Dallas?"

Now I knew Dally hated being called Dallas. She didn't like being named after a place she'd never been, from a woman she didn't remember. But I detected a slight nod.

The woman looked unsteady so I scooted over and she took my seat. I was sitting next to Dally's mom, something I never thought would happen. Not in all the years I knew Dally. We'd spent too many nights wondering about our mamas, mine being somewhere in the afterlife, and hers being in a perpetual state of addiction. I never thought Dally would forgive her enough to seek her out, not after what Dally went through in her foster care families. But time can be enough for some people. I reckon not everyone holds a grudge like I do.

Kendra seemed to have a speech prepared, as if she knew this day would come. In fact, she said she couldn't serve anyone around our age cause she'd drill holes into them searching for

Dally's face. Kendra was barely sixteen when she had Dally, though she looked like a woman who'd seen twice as much in her lifetime. She asked about Dally's upbringing, and I wondered how deep Dally would go into it. Dally got abused by the first family who took her, then stayed with a family of religious zealots until she drifted into an abusive relationship I pulled her away from. For all Dally had been through, you wouldn't know it looking at her. You either sink or swim in life, which sounds real simple, I know. But sometimes people try to make it more complicated for a whole pile of reasons that have nothing to do with living.

Turned out it was hard not to like Kendra. She was as excited to see Dally as you could hope for, and I saw where so many of Dally's mannerisms came from, which was surprisin' seeing how they didn't grow up together. Sometimes there's no villain to point a finger to, and that's a much harder lot to deal with. You can sink your teeth into a villain, gather enough rage to justify bad things. Truth is many things in life are a series of unfortunate events and may require a dulling of your sensitivities just to survive.

Kendra had me thinking about my own mama, how I could never tell who Mama liked or didn't until they walked away. She'd flash her pearly whites and cuss their name later talking about keeping her powder dry. Then she told me about an old bastard we knew in town named Harry. He was a council member, fixing to shut down the only woman's health clinic in town. One night, Mama took me for a drive and stopped in front of his house, then quietly slashed his tires in his driveway. When she got back in the car, she told me to never speak of it. I found out later he was late to his own proposal and it didn't pass by one vote. No one ever suspected her. I started wishing I got the better parts of my mama like Dally did.

We ate our huge pancakes with Kendra while another server covered for her. Well, I did all the eating. Dally was too busy talking. When I was done I excused myself so they could be alone together.

"Dally, I'll be in the truck. Take your time."

When Dally came out a half an hour later, she was holding a Styrofoam container of food.

"You want to talk about it?" I asked.

"Not yet," she said.

"You ready to go then? I gotta get out of this godforsaken state."

She nodded.

I started up the engine and Old Blue purred. We drove through Fort Worth again listening to sad country songs, and just when we hit the city limits I saw the blue and red lights behind me sending me in a panic because I'd made sure I stuck to the speed limit and gave no cause for trouble.

"Dally, if I show him my license and he looks it up, I'm in trouble. Switch with me now!"

"I can't switch with you!" she said, snapping out of her deep thoughts.

I began signaling like I was pulling over and yelling at Dally to take the wheel.

"He'll see us, Clemie! Just act calm and hide your gun."

"A gun is the least of my problems in this state," I said. But I took my sweatshirt between us and stuffed it on the side of the door. "I think I'm gonna be sick." The whiskey and pancakes were churning in my stomach, creatin' something sour. Sure enough, as soon as I pulled the truck onto the shoulder, I opened the door and emptied the content of my stomach. I figured it would make a nice distraction, but you know how cops are. The man just said, "Rough night? License and registration." And while I'm fumbling about for my license he starts commenting on the content of my puke.

"Do I detect some pancakes in the pile of vile?"

Dally leaned over and said, "Not just any pancakes, but the world's biggest."

"You in Dallas at Mabel's Diner?"

"Yes, sir," she said, turning on her charm, which I was mighty grateful for seeing how I ain't got any.

"I love that place!"

"My mama works there. You know Kendra?"

"You bet! Prettiest waitress there."

I stopped fumbling for Yotes' registration because now the cop turned into a pile of soft butter, purring about how he always stopped to see Kendra and so on and so on and my my my how Dally was just as beautiful as she was, and I don't care what no one says, sometimes a nice set of tits and some pearly whites will get you out of a world of shit.

I handed him Yotes' registration. "The way you two look, thought you might have been caught in that tangle last night at Billy Bob's," he said, chuckling. "Rumor was a big fight was started by two pretty ladies matching your description and color of your truck."

"Now you're wrong there," I said. "No one ever accused me of being a lady."

He lost his smile then and said he'd be right back.

"You could've let me drive," Dally said.

"I already told you, Yotes said only me." Of course, I never mentioned to him my run-ins with the law.

"And stop being confrontational," she added.

"I ain't being confrontational! He had no reason to pull us over and he knows it." I adjusted my rearview mirror to watch him. While Dally and I squabbled, the cop came back and interrupted us.

"Seems you're no stranger to the law, Ms. Ferguson."

"Officer," Dally said, sweetly. "I made her come to Texas to see my mama, sweet Kendra, who you know and love, and my friend here knew it was risky, but she's the best friend I've ever had, or will ever have, and she's been behaving the whole time."

I gave Dally a little pinch on the arm for that.

"Tell you what, you promise to head straight home to Arizona I'll let you go with a warning."

"Absolutely!" she said.

"Don't worry officer," I said. "I ain't ever comin' back to this state. It's as flat as those pancakes I couldn't keep down. Hardly a mountain here worth my attention."

You'd think that made the man happy, but he soured on me and gave a wink to Dally.

"Why do all our outings end with cops?" I said pulling back on the highway.

"What are the chances he knew my mama? And that he said I look like her?"

"From the size of his belly, he was no stranger to the world's largest pancakes," I said, digging in the armrest for a stray cigarette Yotes might have stashed.

"Clemie, you can't tell me that wasn't kismet!"

"I'd tell you it wasn't but you wouldn't believe me." I pointed at the glove compartment. "Any cigarettes in there?"

She looked quickly and brushed me off, still distracted at the sheer amount of luck we encountered.

"It was our bracelets with the evil eye that warded him away," she said, reaching into her bag. She pulled out a cigarette and lit it for me. Then she began fumbling with the radio, trying to find my song again. But the thing is, I didn't need a song, let alone two. Daryl was never the reason I went all that way. Truth was, any time I got stagnant, I needed to get in a vehicle and just go, and there was no one I wanted to be with more than someone who knew all the parts of me that didn't need explaining.

"You gonna stay in touch with your mama?"

"She's been clean close to a couple years now." Dally nodded yes and smiled. "I didn't expect to like her so much."

"You came from her, didn't you? Of course she was gonna be sweet! Sweet don't mean you never mess up in life. Look at me! Sweet as shit and I'm on parole." I took a long drag and threw the cigarette out the window.

"When does that end? Your parole?" Dally asked, drilling her eyes in my direction. I didn't answer. In the distance I could see the welcome sign for New Mexico and I was gunning for it like I couldn't get out of Texas fast enough.

"Next month," I said, finally, when we passed the sign.

"Now why would you be taking risks when you only have a month left? You afraid of it ending?"

"What kind of question is that?"

"It's the right kind of question to be asking Clementine Ferguson."

Damn that Dally for knowing where to root around. I got paroled in Phoenix and it kept me there, but then I could go anywhere and I didn't know what that looked like. When you have something holding you down, you no longer see it holding you back.

"You come live with me," Dally said, breaking the silence. "I got an extra room."

I didn't know if I'd take Dally up on that. I was thinking I might shoot for California. I ain't ever seen the ocean. I wanted to see what that was all about. But the gesture touched me.

"You'd have me?" I asked.

She laughed and started singing my song, crooning about Old Clementine and I sang along with her with so much joy in my heart I couldn't see all the bad that happened before or what might be waiting after.

Sabrina Hicks

Coyote, Bones, Howl

Coyote

The house slept while I stayed up stretching, trying to fit my body into this world, knowing something ancient lives inside me and needs to ease into sleep. It worms its way through my bloodstream. A howl, released with a stretch to hide its strangeness. It is all I can do to stay sane. To hold together these bones that rattle inside me, seeking to form the perfect posture like the skeleton we had in anatomy class. We called him Hal. Upright and stoic, staying in the front corner of the room to remind us we are not unlike our parents, that we will always run to and away from death. Hal, pulled to the center of the room once a year for a lesson, covered in dust, dust being primarily the dead skin cells of everyone in class, shedding our younger selves. I am stretching three times a day now and sometimes late into night. My bones pop and click in and out of place. I howl along with them when I am supposed to breathe with intention; intention leads me back to the coyote. The one I am always combing the desert for. The one that stopped to stare at me the day I crossed the rocky wash along the foothills. It had borrowed the eyes of my father. The animal didn't leave until I recognized him. Hiya dad, I said, and he trotted away. Satisfied. It was the only time I recognized someone who wasn't fully in his form.

Bones

I told my teacher I would haunt the halls of high school. I would visit his classroom and toss over the desks to scare the kids. Dance a waltz with Hal. He didn't object. He taught long enough to ignore the ramblings of teenagers unable to commit to time. That was long ago and I have not forgotten. I store memories outside my brain. I shove them around my body so they are always moving, so they do not land in corners. My mother leaves post-it's around the house reminding her to shut off the stove. Watch a boiling pot. Unplug an iron. She worries mostly about fire. Maybe she recalls the one that streaked down the mountain, aiming for our house when I was a child. I was outside doing cartwheels until I landed on my arm and broke a bone. She said it wasn't a good time to go to a doctor. There was a fire to worry about. It was heading for our house. Neighbors stood on graveled yards filled with cacti and exchanged bad information that they repeated until it rose into hysteria. But flames never reached our home. The winds turned and burned down Mr. Kowalski's house. Inside were priceless paintings. That's what he told the insurance lady months later. Mr. Kowalski, we knew, had a bad memory. By the time my mother remembered me, my arm had set funny. Two bones no longer moving with fluidity. I do not fault her. She was running away from Hal. I put a post-it note on my refrigerator to remember to follow through on my hauntings. Where I need to be when my soul doesn't have this body to roam mountains or comb the halls of places I have been, where fluorescent lights create dreamlike memories that no longer serve me, but somehow made me be the type of person who follows through on her threats.

Howl

There was a night when a pack of coyotes tore through our neighborhood yipping and crying. No one knew what got into them. (I know this because the next morning a text chain went out remarking on their howls. It was the kind of text chain never meant to solve anything.) They ran up and down our suburban streets. Through yards and driveways until I saw lights in the neighborhood slowly turn on. I pictured neighbors waking, pulling back their blankets and sheets with high thread counts, setting their feet to the ground, their toes searching for something soft to slide into before investigating. They would rub their blurry eyes, thick with sleep, shuffle to their front doors. Maybe they just looked out the window—safer that way. Maybe they even caught sight of their fur in the dark. Or saw the distant view of city lights turned on at odd hours as the coyotes altered the way we would view the blackened shape of mountains. How the moon rolled between them like a polished stone. One neighbor bravely said they had their .45 ready. Another neighbor said the animals were looking for pets to eat. Make sure to never let them out alone in the dark. Make sure you don't leave food out. Make sure you remember to close your garage. To lock your doors. To install motion sensor lights to flood the dark areas around your homes. Flood them with light. Shoot them with rock salt. I wake every morning with my tongue slick with the taste, my fur matted with thorns and moonlight, a howl escaping from somewhere deep inside me.

Acknowledgments

Thank you to Adam Van Winkle for championing my work, for all the care he took in putting together this collection, and making this dream of mine come true. Thank you to my one and only, Stephen. To my first reader and daughter, Marlo Hicks, my son, Hayden, and of course, Marina. I couldn't do this without the support of my amazing family! Thank you to my reader and writer pals: Kelli Short Borges, Rudri Bhatt Patel, Windy Lynn Harris, Stephanie Austin, Sudha Balagopal, and Beth Sherman. To my friend, Liz Burney, who has been a source of encouragement every step of the way. To Lisa Hayes for her keen eye. To the online community of flash writers–the most generous writers out there! And a special thanks to writer, Dan Crawley, who encouraged me to submit this collection to *Cowboy Jamboree*.

To my late father, for being the inspiration for many of these stories, who never failed to encourage me to write even when it was against my better judgement. And my mother, my best friend.

Thank you to the following publications and their editors for featuring many of these earlier versions of my writing:

Eight Seconds (*Reckon Review*), All Water Holds a Memory (*Five South Journal*), Cowboy Titanium (*Cowboy Jamboree*), Synonyms for Extraction (*MoonPark Review*), Little Lady (*Trampset*), When the Cowboy Separates the Calves for Tomorrow's Branding (*Emerge Journal, Best Micro Fictions*), Memorial of Imaginary Lines (*Sunlight Press*), Fire Season (*Pidgeonholes*), Carriage (*Literary Mama*), Coyote Girl (*Necessary Fiction*), Potential (*Stanchion, Best Micro Fictions*), Farrago (*Flash Frog*), Object Permanence (*JMWW Journal*), When We Knew How to Get Lost (*Cleaver Magazine*), Drill (*Matchbook Lit, Wigleaf Top 10*), Where the Brittlebush Bloom (*Third Eye Sockeye Press*), Pioneer Girl (*Bath Flash Fiction*), Saguaro (*100 Word Story*), Pick-Me-Girl (*Tiny Molecules*), Rattlesnakes (*Cowboy Jamboree*), Olympus Mons (*Monkeybicycle*), Scar Tissue (*New Flash Fiction*), My Drugstore Queen (*Milk Candy Review*), Rock Collection (*CHEAP POP*), Buying Raindrops (*Atlas and Alice, Best Small Fiction*), Writing Prompts and Changing Views (*X-R-A-Y*), Extraterrestre (*Barren Magazine, Wigleaf Top 10*), Dead

Sabrina Hicks

Animal Pick Up (*Bending Genres*), To Arizona (*Third Point Press*), Where the Hummingbirds Go (*Ellipsis Zine*), If Only I Could Tell You (*Synaesthesia Magazine*), Home of Specimen Gardeners (*Barren Magazine*), Blink (*2016 Writer's Digest Grand Prize Winner*), Succession (*Maudlin House*), There Is No Advice I'd Give My 16-Year-Old Self (*Exposition Review*), Walking Contradictions (*Split Lip Magazine*), The Shedding Process (*Pithead Chapel*), Coyote, Bones, Howl (*Fractured Lit*).

www.ingramcontent.com/pod-product-compliance
Lightning Source LLC
LaVergne TN
LVHW091248110826
845146LV00001BA/364